Sky Lord

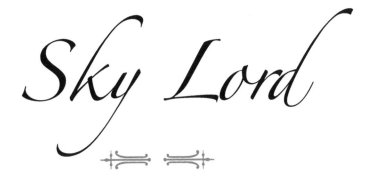

Sky Lord

Original Story

ASYA SHMARYAN

ISBN: 978-1-64921-235-1   (Paperback Edition)
ISBN: 978-1-64921-236-8   (Hardcover Edition)
ISBN: 978-1-64921-234-4   (E-book Edition)

Book Ordering Information

Phone Number: 347-901-4929 or 347-901-4920
Email: info@globalsummithouse.com
Global Summit House
www.globalsummithouse.com

Printed in the United States of America

PART - I
NIGHT AFTER FUNERAL

Chapter 1

AT least twelve years earlier. This story opens-up in the late 1980s or early 90s, of the XX-Century.

At this moment of time, its late afternoon, where came into sight a classy car was driving on a rocky road of Swiss Alps.

Later on, before the night landed, a car has driven by some strangers', when starts descending.

In time this car began climbing, are speeding up, driving to mountaintop that repose, where Switzerland was bordering with Italy. Seeing this car's pursuing a man and a woman, which are in the age of thirties, driving luxury automobile.

The vehicle has driven as a minimum ten miles on narrow road of the Mountains. It seems a car with those strangers is trying overtaken in front this couple's vehicle.

The pair's auto meanwhile, erratically breaks, which made noises that, resonated far afield.

Seen a few hours pass, by now is sundown, and the vehicle kept driving, following this be another car through unsafe road, towards remote.

A man driver in this pair's car is accelerating; seen it's a manual-car with four gears, by, which he's struggling to control the wheel, when maneuver and drive faster.

Seen the car goes ascending, is chasing this pair car, whose speedometer has shown: 90 km. 95 km. 100 km, and it keeps climbing high.

The pair's vehicle tried getting away, driver kept pressing on gas; where someone in a car saw was pursuing them for quite a while. It's emerged be life-threatening situation for this couple.

Suddenly from a pursued car someone starts shooting at the pair's car-tires, while chased them.

Another of the chases is worried: "Stop rotating wheel, it makes me nervous, Ralph!"

At some stage of this pair getaway, the man kept speeding; seen from a chased car they've already fired few times at him or her, simultaneously it's followed them.

Due to wet weather, it was dangerous traveling on the road; this has made the pair to delay. So, the man pressed auto breaks, yet triggered their car off disruption; seen it's been shaken. It's heard the car has made noises, which resonated far and wide.

The driver become conscious of creepy tricks by a chasing car; and tried to bring to a halt his vehicle.

Erratically he is unable to cling to controls of his car-wheel. The car still was on high speed, when on its own accord, engine stops functioning; pair's car is slowly plunging. Seem from deep thrash stones are just about trailing, and steppingstones that kept jointly the foothill, began collapsing...

Activated by force's hunt, this couple's vehicle by clear-fell like it flew from the mountains; and dropped on stone surface; where on be immobile, then car burst in flames.

A few days later, came into sight the streets of London, where have developed a nasty day; and it was raining a whole week, without stop.

Half-hour ago sunrise has loomed over London, where seem been cutting through a mist; where to opens up a view on local Cemetery. There have witnessed burial processions of a married couple: Mr. and Mrs. Dalton. They've died few days ago, in a car accident, in the Swiss Alps. Those deceased couple had left behind two juvenile children: a daughter Christina, and their younger son Aaron.

In a twinkle of an eye, these two coffins have been laid to rest down into the ground: "Down dust to dust, ashes to ashes…"- In a monotone voice declared the priest.

Meantime, Christina's sobbing; before turning her back on Aaron; at the same time, she stares down on the grave, where their parents have been put to rest.

Later that day, when nightfall reached peripheral, it's felt cold; and developed into the darkest night, which persons have ever experienced.

The moon vanished over clouds, but the stars are sparkling in Atmosphere by, which have created patterns across the sky; and the view appeared superb.

At present comes into sight Dalton's mansion, located in the heart of London. In the house be heard seldom bangs, every hour; seen a glow from the moon that fell through the window, directly on a Grandfather's clock.

While, in Dalton's living room be displayed scrawl local stat with collections of newspapers and glossy magazines, laid on coffee table that made of mahogany.

In the middle of the room people's eyes have caught a stock-still fireplace, in which burned firewood.

Revert of the deceased Mr. and Mrs. Dalton who have belonged to aristocratic descendants; but on this particular night in dynasty home came into view those persons are grieving for mister Dalton and his wife, Margaret.

Meanwhile, those remaining guests' have got a chance to munch all they can eat, which was perfectly arranged at the tables, after the funeral procession.

Because of the grief in this family, all mirrors in the house were stayed hidden, and covered over with textiles.

Those guests eyes would frequently catch a man, roughly 1 m 78 cm tall, who happens be of an African or Hispanic appearance, named J.D. Crofter.

He seems is in his late thirties; with medium haircut, black like a crow's wing curly hair, have dark shiny eyes; been seated apart from others on a leather chesterfield. Crofter looks is dressed in dark color piece of a suit; underneath he wore a creamy stylish long-sleeve shirt, with a tie that has matched his outfit.

In the room appeared another chap, a middle-aged man Ralph Bickering; he is in the age of his late forties; has an average size complexion. He has round, like owl-faded eyes; seems him been roughly 1m 70 cm or taller. Ralph is seated in a second wing chair, on opposite side of the room; dressed in a three-piece suit. Underneath his outfit glanced he's wearing an elegant snowy-white shirt that it fastens with a tie. He's present on behalf of J.D., and happens be Crofter's business partner, in the Law Firm.

On other side of the room, guests' eyes have caught a boy. He is the late Mr. and Mrs. Dalton's son Aaron: around eight years old; is fair-haired; and has blue-gray-eyed. He is seated down on carpet, up on a silk pillow, and built a house out of kids' toy blocks.

Close to him came into view a cute fair-haired girl, with similar look to her brother, has blue-eyed; this is Aaron's sister. Christina a bit older than him, and she is roughly ten years old.

Yet Christina stood close to a leather couch, and takes her dices, being playing with this; but she doesn't pay attention to her younger brother.

In the easy chair near the fireplace, and above its tiled mantelpiece lies a book, where seen looking sternly over her glasses, is seated an elderly woman.

She is those orphan broods nanny, wearing a black lace headdress that covers her silver hair, and doing her knitting.

Over two hours later, one of the Lawyer's mister Bickering opens the heavy door; he then invited those guests to go in the room that, be made into a Library, there is going to be reading of those late Mr. and Mrs. Dalton's "Will".

Almost immediately, from the Library perceived Ralph's monotone voice, when he began reading the late couple last wish:

"The deceased George and Margret Dalton have left behind two juvenile children Aaron, and Christina. According to the 'Will', all the entire grand Real Estate that belonged to mister George Dalton and his wife, with the lion's share of their movable, was passed to their younger son, Aaron Dalton!"

Few weeks pass, now minutes ago have developed fascinating view on a sapphire crack of dawn.

At this moment in London Center, appeared an ancient building: this is a Notary Firm, situated, where the Center and King William Street meet near St. Mary's Church; and where saw in a niche displayed a statue of 'Madonna with a child'.

On the outset, came into sight two men: J.D. Crofter and Ralph Bickering are eager to enter the building.

After one of them opens the front door, and let the other man to barge in. Crofter then carefully looks around, makes sure no one was shadowing them.

Next J.D. does follow Ralph. Seen both have vanished behind a heavy door, as they got in.

Upon returning to the office both the Lawyers sit down into leather chairs, on opposite side of the room, but close by, and facing each other. This was a well-known Lawyers firm, specializing in matters: of the Will, inheritance or Guardianship, and dealing with many families' fortunes.

Bearing in mind that Crofter and Bickering would take only wealthy clients. No wonder they're having made themselves competitors for anyone's association of envy; although the sizes of their legal fees, which they've charged significantly exceeded normal.

Observing Ralph is hissing and coughing in the old office hours; and carried a black, pitted bug case of huge proportions that could fit both of those men's bags.

Besides its captivated folks eyes that Ralph is wearing an old-fashioned frock coat, which wrinkled with a bright shirt underneath, and a tie that matched his outfit.

Shortly after J.D. suddenly has got up of his sit, and left, while Ralph's spotted, been seated in the office, solitary.

Soon, there reappears Ralph Crofter's business partner. Though something has surprisingly struck Ralph.

Getting up of his seat, he hurried to the window, where sneaks a peek, and been observing a 'Big Ben Clock Tower', on opposite side of the road.

Candidly those men began pursuing rather important matter, as it seems they're hooked on something major.

It's looked been a private office, where came into view screen made of glass that separated both Lawyers from those clerks in bureau.

It seems a partition worked to their advantage. Those Lawyers would be willingly talking to one another of secret affairs in this Law Firm.

This could keep track of the employees' progress without fear of those officials' ears to get fundamental information for them.

J.D. and Ralph could seldom say a little, but understood each other perfectly. See they're wearing similar outfits, like twin brothers; but they haven't been blood related, quite the reverse.

For a moment they were tongue-tied. Eventually J.D. breaks the silent; it looks him been grumpy; the truth of the matter is that he's tense: "That murky cloud over London, and smoke in the air, with a loud sound of the Church Bells and Big Ben Clock, drowned me insane, again and again!"

To cut his word short, Ralph's raised eyebrows, and have stirred; yet he is whispering: "Oh, back off!

'We've to be worried about something else, if the boss finds out…" He's befallen silent; next Ralph upstretched his hands, as if it's a crucial matter:

"That we live as a couple, he can make working our ass off, even more than ever!"

Hearing of such honest account of projection, Crofter looks as if he's lost at sea.

Those two were seated for a while, without saying a word. To delay J.D began reading letters that he's grabbed from the office.

After finishing with correspondence, J.D. fixed his mysterious corner of an icon; and handed letters to Ralph, for analysis. Once Ralph has read carefully the letter of appeal, ensuing he's nodded his head. He then wrote a resolution for those clerks to proceed.

Only in rare cases their opinions were divergent or fragmentary. It would take them only a few short phrases to understand each other's thoughts. Seeing their expressions ultimately would be recite: and they could come to an agreement.

Crofter began feeling bored, to cheer him up Ralph turns radio on, where a man's voice is broadcasting: "We're reporting news on latest development of the exchange rates…"

Still J.D. didn't listen to the news: seem this radio was only a cover up for them to deceive those clerks that have seated on other side of the partition wall. Apparently this time around, it was pretty important for both Lawyers to talk about, and a partition wall prevent from anyone to hear a single word, whatsoever Ralph and Crofter would say to each other in secret.

Promptly Ralph's stared at J.D. with his round, like an owl, faded eyes. It's about Crofter and Bickering's old client an aristocrat, landowner and a manufacturer, mister Dalton and his wife, who had died a few weeks ago, and deceased left behind two juvenile children. From the time when those Lawyers become guardians to Aaron and Christina, and both broods have remained so far. Those Lawyers are mutually agreed coming-up with schemes to get hold of that fortune for them alone.

A sudden idea came out of space into Crofter's mind; and he slants his head; then began pointing to the door, as a sign for them to go outside.

At this moment Bickering initiated talking, but is whispering: "Okay Crofter, let's go outside, and talk about it?"

J.D in his turn nods his head; and without losing time, he gets up of his sit, first.

Following him is Ralph. At that instance they've grabbed their coats, and left the office.

Once they've stepped outside, ended up on a noisy street; Crofter is into talking:

"Ralph, in case of Aaron's death, and before he is going to reach the age of eighteen, the entire Estate would be reassigned to his sister? Consequently, it would be the end of our guardianship to them? It'll predict even earlier than we can anticipate, on Christina reaching majority age?" He stops talking; takes a deep breath; and is ongoing: "This Bank gave us a supplementary on depositors of having their mails sent to them or held at the Bank itself. Verifying that there're no traces of the account, as they listed. Rarely Bank nominates next of kin. Private banking clients apart from not nominating next of kin, by, which usually in most cases, leave the 'Will' in our care; he could die be unheard." Crofter became silent for a minute; this has initiated, Ralph remained idem.

In short, not completed verses, which have meant only one thing: both of them want to get rid of Aaron, for good.

Chapter 2

MANY days later, it's mid-morning in London, where the sky covered with gray clouds, appears been an indication of a rainstorm. There's not far from Downtown of London arisen a construction site, where seen the workers are building anew skyscraper.

Open-air appears a Ralph Bickering sits beside J.D. Crofter, in nearby Park, on the bench. Ralph seems is excited by J.D. suggestion: "Croft, I thought about your idea, and you're right! Legally it is possible for Aaron to appear insane? And it would be recognized by an established order." Has assumed Bickering.

For those dexterous trustees, the situation was in their favor. Contrary for Aaron, who would be alive, but vanish, thus it would be a risk for him reaching the majority age?

So far the idea to put Aaron in a mental health Institution for neurological children haven't left those Lawyers minds.

J.D. and Ralph have focused they're arrangements, which would involve Dalton's fortune. Paying special attention to details, those Lawyers-guardians decided upon Aaron's fate: o'er it has run into the money.

Ralph directly brings to light matter, but it would involve hurdles: 'And we can proceed, without anyone is suspicious.

'In fact, I've searched for orphanages or I should say Monastery, and found one, it's in Chinese province of Tibet. There're more agreeable people. I know, it's a gamble, but for us it would be achievable. I can tell you even more, today I've received a telegram, from that Monastery.' Ralph bends head down; sees is holding a telegram; he then began reading it. After finished, he raises his head, and passes the letter to J.D. to read it. Be motivated, Ralph begun chew the fat: "This Institution represents a great benefit for us. China is far away, and so are the tutorial authorities. By, which you and I will be living prosperous, without any problems,"- he stops talking briefly; is taken a deep breath. Next Ralph's putting a grin, and is ongoing: "J.D. I've requested a report from the Bank, and they specified of a condition depositing capital on Private banking affairs, those who patronize their services prefer anonymity. Don't forget with some levels of detachment from conventional processes. Nevertheless, in their system Aaron will remain no next of Kin!"

Crofter agreed to this; yet is reacting wisely: "You're right, Ralph! And yet, we wouldn't allow Christina to see her little brother growing up, alongside her?"

As a minimum two weeks have passed, since. In this moment of time inactivity be seen on London streets, where have developed a tight climate with snowfalls. The blizzard was wild for days without stopping, subsequently the surface ground been covered thoroughly with snowflakes, the sky noticed developed overcast.

Meanwhile, there was a prompt visit to the Lawyers office, where it's witnessed one of those Solicitors.

Bickering is typically hissing and coughing, in the old office hours. Seem it's as usual he has pitted his bug case of such huge proportions that could fit both his and Crofter's things.

Constantly through partition Ralph and J.D., by logic for their safety, they could maintain discussions in private, particularly from those nosy ears and eyes.

Up-to-the-minute Ralph and Crofter said very little to each other, since they've already decided how to proceed. Both appear are dressed in similar colors costumes, as they would typically prepare.

Crofter breaks silent, is complaining; he's looking nervous when snapped: "The snowstorm with overcast around London, have made me nearly losing my mind!"

Ralph cuts his speech; and alone began mumbling; seen he is uneasy: "Butt off, Croft, don't be grumpy! We've to worry about more important things: what if someone finds out about our plans?" Yet Ralph became silent; and raised his hands up. He then lows hands down; and is closed them on his chest:

"That we're going to put Aaron in a mental health Institution? Not only we both can kiss goodbye to our careers, but will end up in jail?"

Hearing of that reason, J.D. has turned stone white on the spot. They're seated for a while silently, and staring.

Crofter, meanwhile, began reading correspondences. Once he has finished reading it; he's fixed his mysterious corner of an icon.

After J.D. has handed the correspondences to Ralph, who's begun reading them too. This time their opinions were analogous, and right away they come to an agreement. As always, J.D. didn't listen to the news, because the television was a deception for those snooping clerks.

For J.D and Ralph it was essential to read the Will again; both one after, the other checked the file: according to what's written in there, the entire Real Estate that young Dalton inherited from his late parents.

As Lawyers purpose was to seize this great fortune for themselves, in which a child could keep it all, by dint of those guardians were influenced by greed and jealousy.

On a Crofter slants his head, as a sign to the door; and is mumbling: "Ralph, let's go outside, and talk about it?"

Ralph in his turn nods his head, and gets up of his seat. Next Crofter is following him. They are having grabbed their coats as usual; and left the office.

Immediately after they've stepped out on open-air, Ralph's expression shown of a thrill, when he began talking: "This guardianship is a real Gold Mine! Imagine, in how many industries we'll invest? You can do business with important person?"

"Substantial! With that source of income we'll get rich!" Supported him Crofter.

Many days have passed, since the Lawyers decided on boy's future. Right this moment, in Dalton's mansion, seen Aaron is seated in the lounge room, restlessly waiting for J.D., who's opened up to him, earlier on: "Aaron, you and I are going on a trip. Go now and pack up your things, because we're leaving England, in a few days!"

Been simply a naive child it has not sunk to Aaron at first, whereabouts J.D. taken him? Besides, he seems is confused, but speechless; without losing a sec. Aaron is asking him: "Sir, please, tell me, where we are traveling to?"

Crofter determined for this boy to pack up basic things, which he must bring, and is advised: 'Aaron, take only few necessary things. You required bringing a toothbrush with toothpaste, blanket, jumper, warm cloths, hat, and a coat. Don't forget to bring with you a pair of rubber gumboots, because we will be wearing this!'

Resultant of his and Ralph's decision, J.D. booked tickets earlier for him and Aaron on a vessel that should navigate them both across the Pacific Ocean.

Not long after Crofter took this boy with he's packed, small luggage…

Sees Crofter quickly walks off the room, and is dragging along Aaron; then he's closed the door behind, with a key.

It's approached the end of the day; that indicated been on the brink of darkness. Crofter and Aaron have joined other passengers, on this vessel.

Afterward they have settled in the first class compartment for the rich and famous. Aaron's felt urge mixture of excitement, from the time when they've embarked onboard; and he's thinking this will acquire for him new experiences.

When both boarded the ship, they've promptly received the right size of sleeping bags from that crew, to match with other voyagers. Equally both got gears to adapt it sailing alongside voyagers, or use in unforeseen incidents that may occur on the Sea. In case of emergency, or for rescue purposes all the travelers on board would wear a life jacket.

Be in a happy mood, Aaron shared his excitement with J.D.: "Sir, I look ahead of the adventure and voyage that will take me away to unknown countries?"

When their vessel cast off from a pier in Brighton, Aaron's journey has just started. In spite of all negative stories that he's heard, this adventure on the sea came out in contrast to his childlike imagination.

A few days passed into the cruise; Aaron seems is waiting restlessly, when J.D. would tell him where they're traveling to?

It seems for Aaron, who has received personally some kind of lifetime lesson; and not only that, he got a lifebelt jacket too, kid's size, of course.

"For me, it's a duration buoy that I received: a lifebelt in children size, and compulsory equipment for waterway." Has analyzed all these gears this boy.

Visiting the storeroom, where see compulsory gears for sea voyage were kept. It was exciting with new experiences for Aaron, and he's been looking ahead to endeavor on a vessel that will take him away to the continent-wide countries.

Once the ship entered 'the open sea', Aaron become scared, and demanded: "Sir, please, take me back to my nanny, and Christi at once!"

Crofter contrary wasn't friendly, and responded in a harsh voice: "Shut up! Our vessel has already entered the open sea. And nobody, do you hear me, nobody will turn back the ship to shores, just for you!" J.D. then began explaining plainly everything to this boy.

After a while Aaron began feeling sick, on the spot whined to J.D.: "Sir, I can't stay still? I'm traumatized due to a storm, because it's thrown me from side to side!"

As a child, with a slim build constitution, Aaron couldn't walk, without be unbalanced; still jointly he's stepped on ship's upper deck. So he was afraid, and yet demanded: "I want to see my mother and father!"

Crofter promptly responded, being angry: "Your parents are not a life!"

It seems Aaron's on the point of crying: "Then I want to see Christina!"

Despite, there have occurred a minor storm in the Pacific; it was Aaron's first experience on a vessel, in contrast to what he has learned from his favorite Fairy tales, which their nanny read to him and Christina.

Later, saw Aaron was on the brink of puking, and almost collapsed: "Mr. Crofter, I've been vomiting constantly a whole day, and it keeps emerging. I feel sick, and my head is spinning round."

It's immediately given the impression that Crofter didn't pay attention to the boy's condition; contrary he thought: "Taken into consideration it would be good for us, if Aaron dies now? Then Ralph and I couldn't bother to pay all the bills to keep Aaron in that Institution? Both of us will then seize his fortune, and spend on Stock Exchange, or into other businesses?"

Be cunning, before anyone can realize, J.D. harshly told him: "Aaron, put yourself together, and don't complain! Is that understood?"

Despite being unwell off seasickness, Aaron felt pressured; he bows head down, and is reacting: "Yes, Sir! Can I have a glass of water, please?"

Somehow other ship voyagers' noticed that Aaron was sick, and they've become concerned for his health.

A few passengers decided to report about Aaron's condition, especially when a child was involved, directly to the ship's Captain.

Later an Italian couple entered Aaron's cubicle, and gave him tablets to help from seasickness. This Italian woman sat down on boy's bed, is stroking his hair. Be emotional, she hugged this boy to make him calm down, put a smile for Aaron, who's felt warm-heartedness.

After the woman left his cubicle, her husband remained for a chat: "My boy, I love the sea, and so is that crew from the ship. As much as we all adore water, from time-to-time it makes us feel awful, mostly when there's a storm and it shakes the sea."

Though Aaron was in no humor to ask this couple: since all was new to him, mainly words those men used, haven't sunk to a child's mind: "Sorry, sir, but I care about my own health!" Reacted Aaron.

In a difficult situation, later Crofter asked him: "Aaron, do you really feel that bad, and couldn't hold on, until we get to China?"

This boy anxiously primed: "No sir, I'm feeling very sick, help me, please! I can't wait till… Are we really traveling to China?" Be amazed Aaron, and forgotten about seasickness for a moment.

A while after, this Italian couple has reappeared in front of Aaron, and offered him tablets that were sort of remedy from seasickness.

Aaron looks confused; and doesn't comprehend what was going on. On the spot those Italians have explained: "Don't be, Aaron, scared, these certain tablets for people, who were at the sea for the first time, or whom a cruise have caused seasickness."

Aaron was naive and a trusting child has swallowed given tablets.

It seems this Italian couple be fond of Aaron, but worried about the boy's state of health.

Almost immediately, they became devoted to him, and would spend great amount of time to take care of Aaron.

From time to time the Italian couple come-up on upper deck; next they moved under, to ship's Captain cubicle to inquire on Aaron's condition.

In next to no time, Aaron's health has improved; though he become more relaxed, and even being able to evaluate the situation.

Two days pass into crossing, Aaron was feeling well. His anxiety has vanished; now he is thinking: "For me floating on waterway, it's fantastic!"

Chapter 3

OVER two weeks have gone, from the time when J.D. and Aaron boarded a vessel from England Seaport, been prearranged as they sailed for the country of China.

A few weeks into cruising was concluded; there saw Crofter alongside Aaron have disembarked in Chinese Tibet.

While Crofter's plan was relocating Aaron to certain facilities, which officially didn't exist on papers; yet, this was a Monastery or mythical Institution for the neurotic children. Nonetheless, Aaron was ignorant of it.

Later that day, in Monastery's office emerged Crofter is talking to Dens Fiend. Here came into view Brian Evildoer, the Monastery's Head of Studies, in which appear they're making arrangements about Aaron's future.

Anyhow, J.D. is not shocked that paperwork began immediately, and he's initiated on talking: "Thank you, gentlemen, for accepting Aaron in your Monastery!"

On a whim Dens Fiend handled the situation alone, in some sort of superior manner: "Happy to oblige. However, we demand of you to change this boy's name, he must be called in a Chinese name!"

Crofter directly interrupts him; seems he is calm, cool and collective, yet contradictory: "I didn't see this coming. Is it necessary?"

Fiend nods his head; and promptly tells more: "Oh, yes, it is! Don't forget you're in China! Therefore, we need to change the boy's name to a Chinese one. Do you have an idea, what you wish him to be called?"

J.D. is astonished, but well mannered. Fiend's contrary impulsive: "I repeat, what name you're having in mind for him, mister Crofter?"

Crofter thinks for a minute; and has come back with: "Well, if that's the case? We thought of his name Xian Wei!"

In a flash Evildoer is interfering; as he seems be stunned: "Why, he's to be called Xian Wei?"

J.D. places a grin, angles his head to make a point: 'Fellows, my business partner and I are Aaron's guardians! And we've decided that he'll remain in China for long time. Since there're rules here to be obeyed, in which he must be called by a Chinese name; and what a better resolution to name him Xian Wei?'

This time Fiend gets up of his seat, and is in motion.

Shortly, are witnessed Crofter and Fiend: money changed hands between them.

In time, near the Monastery be added a building Hospital so as to increase number of those adapts alongside Monks, for certain covert regulations.

In facilities, meantime, they've prepared those broods for their future as Monks, to be Teachers of Buddha in Asia.

Those so-called miracles workers are having experimented: medium, hypnotists, with other tests: such as aura, for instance by, which they forced the pupils to learn unrevealed 'occult knowledge'.

At some stage of preparations seniors' scholars would show fighting discipline that they're trained in for spiritual ceremonies; or being involved teaching those youngest to become the future Monks.

Although, this Institution has existed unofficially, yet only guardians, relatives, or those who for some reasons, want to get rid of the child, would place them in that Institution.

Barring in mind the Monastery staffs, simply have stolen many of those broods from their parents battling throughout China; and been extended their wicked conducts in there.

More often than not, those scholars and 'scientific advisers' would have become evident of many talented individuals among pupils in this Institution, with super great knowledge. But this monastery, one of the foundations in Social system, by, which they were having served and preached Buddhism.

In time, it's become doomed; in a view of this had lost its charm amongst those masses, because got a blow.

In order to describe teachers in Monastery apart from the Monks, it's more proper to label them 'Masters of Buddha'.

They've come here from all over Europe, many of them from Britain; several people among the Teachers on their own accord, or maybe not?

Dens Fiend and Brian Evildoer, for instances were not Buddhists. From the time when they had left Britain, and reached Tibet, both were having worked in the same field: religion.

Wished-for the Christian faith this method has belonged to kind of foundation in the social system that Fiend and Brian formed.

It's appeared that Evildoer's duty was the Head of studies there, while Fiend being in charge of these staffs.

Together they've run the Monastery, and called themselves 'Masters' on behalf of Buddha; despite Fiend and Brian weren't Monks both fooled around those locals.

One of those days, during their discussion, Brain seems be worried, when got hold of Fiend: "Dens, what we're going to do with those talented students?"

Fiend in contrast, is talking without showing irritation: 'Hypnosis must be given, my friend, especially to talented one, which are the most nervous students. Only this will work and keep them under control. Trust me, this method was practiced in some places around China, even all over India. For the same purpose it'll be served with all kinds of tricks: like the luminous halo around the body of fragrances. 'Despite experimental purposefulness, it's being invisible to others such as their lips movements, brainpower, eyes, and voices sound: all these have been aimed for miracles, which we'll achieve, as their mentors!'

Seems Evildoer has taken a moment to bend down; and gave a shake with his head; he still is uncertain: "What if it doesn't work, Dens? In that case, we need a backup plan, don't you think?"

Now Fiend intrudes; alone says-so: "There were involvement of scientific advisers, and tried this; nevertheless these surrogates for the same purpose, with all kinds of tricks.

Over all extreme aggravation of receptivity, these will allow certain scholars serve as readers of thoughts.

Among the substitutes who have to maintain faith in deity, spirituality, could support of a mystical mood."

Evildoer nods his head, as if convinced: "In that case, I allow you to prepare!"

Chapter 4

SO incoherently twelve years had passed, from the time when Aaron parted with his sister; and disembarked in a forsaken part, where Chinese Tibetan Buddhist Monastery existed.

Present-day Aaron sat on the floor in the yoga position, near the window in his chamber, which remind more of a prison-cell.

A table there, chair, single-bed with a metal bedrail and a rug spread to the corners that has made up altogether the furniture. The window looked out into the courtyard, where be dull and silent. Neither a scrub, nor a blade of grass sand and gravel is like a corner of a desert island, enclosed by prison-like walls of a gloomy building with small windows.

The tops on the trees of the dense park surrounded the Institution represented above the raised roofs, which wasn't unusual for a Buddhist Monastery.

A tall brick fence divided the park and Monastery structures from outside world.

Deep silence was broken only by the creak of gravel under the leisurely steps by those teachers that were on behalf of Buddha and those educators.

Those pupils were brought to this Institution from all over the world, and placed in the same wretched rooms as Aaron's chamber was.

Among them were eight-year-old and fully-grown girls and boys. They've made up a family.

Except for their quiet and mean words, in their eyes, which weren't difficult to notice, neither love. Nor friendship, or affection was permitted, and not joy at get-together, rather sorrow at parting with each other.

From the very first days of schooling in the Monastery, these feelings eradicated from students and followers, in all measures by educators, teachers over pressure: Fiend and Evildoer that were Englishmen.

Help of restraining those pupils' by hypnotists, which were Europeans, primarily English, and the occultists of new formations.

Aaron called Xian Wei, meanwhile, appears wearing a tunic short-sleeved shirt with a brown overcoat made of thick fabric. There're not even tumbled on his feet. To describe Aaron: he is seemingly tall, fair-haired man, but is clean-shaven bold, around twenty years. Although by the expression on his face he could sometimes be given less: light-grayish eyed he looked with childlike simplicity; but light wrinkles were already visible upon his high forehead, like a person who had suffered a great deal and changed his mind. Color of his eyes and hair indicated that he was of European origin. Aaron has all grown up, seen he's expression with consistent Anglo-Saxon appearance been motionless, like a mask. He stared blankly out of window, when from nowhere a man plunged into his view.

Accordingly it's the mentor Fiend or second 'Master Buddha', who would force Aaron to take stock of the day every evening to remember all the events that occurred from dawn to dusk, like so he tested Aaron's attitude, has checked his thoughts, desires, and actions. Before going to bed, Aaron would give an account to confess to one of educators at what he's mind-sets.

Right this moment, on other part of the world, in England, at Dalton's mansion, at the living room, came into view a man, around 1 m 75 or taller; brunette, with dark blue-eyed. He is in the age of his mid thirties; has a medium-to-short haircut. This is Andrew Greenwood, a private investigator, from the USA.

A minute ago a young woman has entered the room; and walks up to Greenwood; she then is seated near him on this chesterfield.

Andrew rapidly gets up of his seat, and bows his body in respect; while is seeking contact: "Good evening, Miss Dalton!"

Christina places a smile, it seems she is friendly: "Good evening, Mr. Greenwood! Did you have a pleasant flight from America?"

Greenwood smiled once again: "Yes, thank you! I've enjoyed traveling, and flew up here at your request! I was eager to see you, Miss Dalton, when you called me, and said it's an urgent matter?"

Christina in contrast, looks be absentminded; and fidgets: "Yes, it's a matter of life and death for someone, who is very dear to me!"

By hearing her honest account, Greenwood inclines his head, and is listening carefully.

Christina realizes that he's got her attention: and began telling about her childhood: and how she had parted with her little brother...

'That's all I remember about Aaron. I was only a child, back then.'- She stops talking, and taken gulps of air. Seems tears are fixed in her eyes. Next she's indicated: "I've searched whereabouts my brother could be? Sadly, result came with nothing, so far!" She became silent for a jiffy.

Christina then looks at him with hope: "You a private investigator, mister Greenwood, and I want to hire you. Money is not an issue, here."

Andrew instantly cuts her word, and is soliciting: "You can call me, Andrew! It's easier for us to communicate, Miss Dalton!"

Christina nods her head, as an agreement: "Certainly! And don't be official with me! You can call me Christi! Are you hungry, mister, I mean, Andrew? My cook has prepared lamb chops, and I would like to invite you for…"

Andrew interrupts her speech, alone said: "I'm sorry, Miss Dalton, but I'm a vegan!"

Bonding into mutual understanding with him, Christina walks to the chest of draw and took out a box, she then opens it up.

Taken out a photo, she's handed it to Andrew: in this portrait shown a woman, roughly thirty years of age, with sad eyes that drawn everyone to.

Alongside her smugly a smiling burly man, possibly in similar age that wore a frock coat with sash of a blue ribbon.

To keep on arrangement with Andrew, Christina opens a draw in the desk; and takes out a check. Extending her arm, she offers him a signed blank check: "Andrew, take this check it's for your expanses!"

Andrew in a flash appears with a nervy grin; but is quivered his head: "No, Miss Dalton I won't take the money! I've not found anything yet that will interest you."

In hearing this, she began crying. By taken out a scarf from under her sleeve, Christina wipes the tears from her eyes.

Despite of her concern look due to reaction of a photo she's shown to detective; still puts on brave face, is clarifying: "I do trust you, Andrew! And yet, the main obstacles to me for over twelve years ago, particularly when I grew up, I couldn't see my brother, Aaron nurtured alongside me?"

Suddenly, she stops talking; and takes a deep breath. Suddenly Christina began pleading: "I beg you, find my brother, Andrew! He is the only family that have left for me in this world!"

Andrew raises his hands, and is crossed them on his chest: "Miss Dalton, I'll do my best to find him. But I need strong substantial evidence to start the search, from somewhere? Can you give me a hint, at least?"

She thought for a minute, seem tried to recall something. Finally, she proclaims:

"Andrew, try Lawyers Firm, in London downtown, Mr. Crofter and Mr. Bickering are working there.

'They were guardians to my brother and me, after our parents had passed on, thirteen years ago!"

A few days later, it's happened at lunchtime, where on the streets of London have seemed partake many starving people that are seated in a "Teashops", or Bistros.

At this moment, came into view a man, in London's center, is crossing the road.

He is wearing a coat, with a high collar pulled up. This man appears be detective Greenwood, is on foot swiftly, toward those Lawyers office where an old building located.

Two hours later, after they were discussing, which shed light on what's occurred over a decade ago was completed; Andrew has left their office, and the building.

Meantime, Ralph began staring at J.D. with his round, like owl-faded eyes. This was important matter, in which both Lawyers hold a talk, while J.D. gesturing by waving his hands: "What about this detective, what's his name, Greenwood?"

Ralph nods, and takes over the conversation: "Yes. Croft, do you think we've to get rid of him? Before he finds out the whole scam?" He shuts up. By taken a deep breath, he is ongoing:

"No, it's risky! When the Bank gave us selection to depositors of having their mails sent to them. Or held at the depository system itself, ensuring that there are no traces of the account the staffs had listed. Though the Bank wouldn't nominate next of Kin, and be kept the same applicant. Private banking apart from nominating next of Kin was usually preserved loyalty to their clients. In the most cases, leave the 'Wills' in our care. In this case, Aaron would die over there, with no-one new and unheard?"

The next day, in late afternoon, Andrew walks up and down at his hotel-room, but not before he firstly visited those Lawyers Firm earlier. He looks as if is inspired; yet engaged in his thoughts, and is absorbing the situation: "The whole thing seems to be strange? Except for the aspect of Dalton's family fortune remained mystery to me? And what role both Lawyers played in all these? As they've stored in the ledger, behind the thick walls of fireproof cabinet? It's a scam?"

At the same day, when evening has touched upon London, Andrew is seen packing up his most necessary things, and folding them in a portable suitcase, it meant one thing he's going on a trip.

Hour later, Andrew has walked off his hotel room; and closed the door behind, with the key card.

After returning a key-card to hotel's admin, he's forthwith, been stepping out-of-doors, Andrew seems is into his assignment.

It's seen a gloomy night outside, where mist has visited London at this time of the year, covered over the entire sky and beyond.

A few steps away nothing was visible, as Andrew looked into dark that obscured metropolis through a thick fog.

Almost immediately, Andrew's eyes seen a cab; it's driving towards him. Without loosing time, he lifts his arm to stop the cab, is yelling: "Taxi, stop here!"

He's getting in the cab, and is settled at the back sit; then orders the driver: "Take me to Heathrow Airport, please!"

The cab driver rotates, and looks at Andrew through a sill. He then nods his head, is agreeing: "Yes, sir! Right away!"

The driver turns back, and has started car's ignition instantly. Saw the vehicle then began slowly moving ahead, and is gaining speed.

On Andrew's arrival at the Airport, without delay he began searching for the right counter, to purchase an airplane ticket.

Succeeding in finding it; he puts his head in windowsill, and is asking the Airport official, in a sweet-talk voice: "I want purchase a ticket on the earliest flight to China, in economy class seat, please?"

The Airport official in windowsill looks sternly at Andrew; even so, without delay collects cash from him; following she gave a nod; and tosses a ticket back to him.

Three hours later, Andrew has still remained at Heathrow Airport. After visiting the lavatory, he's moved separate from other passengers, been seated on a bench: "I cannot believe my luck, I bought a ticket on airplane? It's only couple hours remained for my departure to China?"

Andrew bends to look at his wristwatch, being excited; and is into thinking. He then is inhaling gulp of air; gets up of his seat, and starts walking to aimed gate.

It had passed few weeks, from the time when Andrew left England; and by now he arrived in China.

Time in-between, still staying put in China, upon his stopovers, Andrew has visited one city after another, all over Chinese mainland.

Yet it didn't prevent him searching for Aaron, ubiquitously; but he found nothing so far that would lead detective Greenwood towards young Dalton.

Another ten days have ended; seen this time Andrew embarked on Tibet; where in this part of China's inland was situated. He resulted to expand his search; on this occasion Andrew has stationed in a grandeur Hotel.

The next day on his arrival, at lunchtime, he's eyes caught a man of Caucasian appearance, who's just entered Hotel lobby, in which Andrew dwelt.

This mysterious looking man is wearing flex shirt, with an elegant outfit, on top a dark hat, and he's medium-to-tall.

Suddenly some thought of intuition drove Greenwood to get a hold of him. Without thinking, detective comes within reach of the admin counter, to where this mysterious man stood; on the spot Andrew is pretending:

"Can anyone help me?"

Spurt stares at him, but being cautious, it looks as if he is passing judgment on a stranger: "What is it that you after, sir?"

Andrew forms a smile, is assumingly: 'Oh, hello, sir! How wonderful to meet someone, who speaks English, and from Europe too? Or am I wrong, sir?'

Spurt extends his hand to shake with Andrew's: "You hit on target! I'm from Europe! My name is Spurt. And what's your name, sir?"

Andrew's reaction spontaneous: "I'm Andy Greenwood! I work as a journalist!"

Spurt seems doesn't trust him, though is responded: "Andy, do you work for a newspaper? And you didn't answer, what are you after?"

Andrew takes a moment to collect his thoughts. When next he proceeds, is said: 'Sir, I've a great deal of money in the Bank, and come to China to spend this. I'm on my way to Hong Kong, however if I find a good deal to make business here? I'll definitely invest in. Can you suggest certain traders?'

On a whim Spurt is amused: "Can I call you Andy? And you can call me Spurt."

Greenwood nods; curves his head forward as if is paying attention to what he intents saying.

Spurt makes a suggestion: "My advice to you is to invest in Chinese Tibet Orphanages, or in Monastery!"

Andrew pretend as if be stunned: "Really? Why is that? What profit will I get from charities?"

This time around, Spurt declared: "I'm a doctor! To be honest, Orphanages need cash flow. And I just happen to know such facilities, where money desperately needed. If you want invest in, this is the best way. I can even take you there?"

On this occasion, as a respect Andrew extends his hand to shake with Spurt: "Yes! I'd like visiting!"

Chapter 5

AT this moment it seems the climate in China be developed frosty but smoggy, since winter visited this forsaken part of the world. Despite cold weather, the sun was shining; while snow sparkled like gems; all in all it's developed a warm day.

Suddenly a minute ago viewed the sky has transformed into mauve crack of dusk.

For the time being, in Tibet's Monastery came into view Fiend, who's called on Aaron to come see him, in one of the Buddhist Convent chambers.

When Aaron crossed the threshold; Fiend without losing a second, began dealing with him: "Xian Wei, according to the Monastery rules the senior Scholars must lead the youngest. Being yourself the first and nearest to the teacher Guru, learn: it's no caring, or friendship to be allowed! It must be only a blind obedience by those junior toward seniors students, that's essential in our education!"

Aaron's, contrary kept in mind liberty, when now and then was playing a fool for the Monastery's staffs, even if him been under pretense of a complete obedience. Was called Xian Wei kept self-preservation, which it's made him hypocritical, and eased Aaron's existence, on many occasions, whilst was ingeniously faking.

He would bear in mind: "Since I've met this boy Song Chuan, and this girl Yuan Lu, I recognized they're smart! They instinctively knew, what was required of them? But this boy was crushed by life! Compare to me, bearing in mind that I'm a foreigner, sternly and spoiled?"

Later, when they're left alone in the chamber, Aaron would whisper to Song Chuan, a student he was teaching, what his thoughts were in Monastery so-called teachers or the Monks that have alarmed him. He often escaped a word Guru, contrary Aaron declared with abhorrence: "How I hate them!"

As this boy knew whom Aaron meant, since he no less has hated Fiend with all of his tormentors. But this boy's feeling was paralyzed by fear. Instinctively he was trembling once heard the Monastery staffs footsteps, looking with fear for himself and for Aaron.

From the time when Song Chuan became friends with Aaron, he called him 'Bo', translated from Mandarin 'brother'. This boy trusted an elder 'brother' with his wicket thoughts: such as delicious cuisine or candies.

Working towards easing this boy's existence Aaron called Xian Wei, was able to achieve a virtuosity trust in the higher rank among Monks; and equally he has led the charade.

At this moment of time climate in the Chinese fields still sensed frost, though it vaporous. Whereas at open air felt winter was coming to an end; seeing the sun shined since this morning, and surprisingly it's a warm day.

Quickly minutes ago, there's appeared a mauve crack of dusk, began covering the entire sky across China. It was one of those nights, as a full moon developed, influenced individuals that have been vulnerable.

This moon movement has affected Aaron that would disappear in fantasy world, with all-inclusive into his childhood memories. In a moment image could turn blurry on its own accord; he's felt as if all around has faded away: eyes are weakening; and Aaron forgets what started years ago.

Visions would affect Aaron mostly at night, he's seen in daydream flyover, in which has reached London across leaden sky, with fancy streetlights; where developed hazy radiance through thick gray-brown fog, it's massive. Surrounds were wet from constant rainfalls, whilst situated seen in damp houses.

People could unexpectedly appear; then would disappear into twilight or mist, or they were relocated to Nightclubs.

It's like Aaron flown in daydream, recalling his childhood, when many years ago he lived in England. He's been seated in the car, looking from a windowsill at the smoky, raw, vague world.

Meanwhile, Andrew sees a different image in his mind, like a fast-forward film: it was in Dalton's mansion; where he's concentrated on a fireplace in family room.

At open-air, the moon vanished from the sky: saw it's glow fell on Grandfather's clock inside, by, which been heard with bangs, every hour: Bang-Bang...

Catching Aaron's reflection, Andrew begun thinking: "I've seen a boy in the room, where Dalton mansion located. He seats on the carpet, and has built a house out of blocks? Nearby sits on a silk pillow, a cute blonde girl, and takes her dice..."

Andrew reflecting intuitively: "Why didn't I realize, they're Aaron and Christina?"

It was flashback of memory for Aaron, as he's imagined what come to his mind...

Meddling with Aaron's daydream, in Dalton's house appeared a man, wearing a suit. On a whim, Andrew is wondering: 'He's an evil man; his round, like the owl eyes are with a disgusting fake smile. What does go into Aaron's mind? Aaron is afraid and hated him. A man in dark suit holds on, and is walking straight on carpet with a false smile; yet in his eyes is seen anger. He's rapidly squashed Aaron's toy house out of blocks, and this fall down! Little Aaron cries out, but this man grabs his arms, and lifts him up...'

Finally Aaron's hallucinations stopped, his dreams have been disrupted. He slowly awakes, and is conscious of those foes. He now has realized they're Crofter and Bickering.

Chapter 6

∽∾∾

MORE time had passed. On this particular day, the sun was in zenith. It seems in Tibet hospital's laboratory within Monastery have been conducting unique experiments.

From nowhere, laboratory entered a young man in his age of twenties, is of a Chinese appearance; with a pale, weary face; wore specs that been concealed. This is Chen Jung, Spurt's assistant. A rumor has it that, doctor Spurt seemed is having a reputation as a genius, in the field of surgery procedures.

Currently in hospital's ward gathering a small group of honorable guests, who came witnessing what, be arranged; and they're intrigued by the situation.

Having idea of his own, one of them Fang Yen stood apart, is seen amid the guests doubted these experiments. And he's suddenly declaring: "In my practice, I've never seen a case of mythical story that you're trying to establish, Spurt? You a Charlatan!"

Resulting he raised his head; voicing an opinion: "Dr. Hui Wei, it's prompted significance of myths by Buddhist Monks that were levitating, in their own time? What you're trying to prove here is impossible?" At this point he halts of talking; is taken a deep breath. Ensuing Fang Yen prolongs, on what his principal be based: "I was born in China, but never heard cases of levitation? Yet, we the scientists' are not ordinary people, but if individual tell me on this kind of experiment he or she being an eyewitness? I would say to them colleagues, you were the victims of a clever deception, or hypnosis!"

Though Spurt interrupts him, in the midst of the speech: "Mr. Fang Yen, and honorable guests, you're still not convinced? Well, we here are not on the Chinese New Year Festival, or in the Circus," Spurt halts talking. He turns around; and is tackling his assistant: "Chen Jung, please, show mister Fang Yen and to all honorable guests, experiment number one!"

To comply with doctor's demand, this assistant walks off to another chamber.

Shortly Chen Jung returns with a tray, in which placed a small dark box, with a key be inserted in. Spurt swiftly turns to face this Chinese man; and is directing him: "Look here, mister Fang Yen! Go and lift up the cover, then open enigmatic box with this key, please!"

Fang Yen resultant to prove he's right, and is turned the key of that box. But he doesn't need to force lifting its cap, Eureka: in front of everyone's eyes it opens under spring pressure: amazingly out of the box arises a light sponge that is flown out, this thing being in the size of a man's fist.

On the spot this metallic mass flew steeply, with a slight thud, then it hits the ceiling; by quirk of fate, thing is stuck to the surface. Witnessing experiment, this Chinese man stood in disbelief.

At the recess, Fang remains astonished; and wrote rather vital in his notebook. He remains confused; and raised his head to look at this fragment that resembles to a sponge, but it's stuck upon the ceiling; by looking closer this's made of a metallic mass. This revelation has puzzled everyone.

Spurt meantime, turns to face his assistant, and is ordered: "Chen Jung, please, bring more things for our second experiment!"

Proceeding doctor's assistant left the laboratory again. Upon his return, Chen Jung brings a stepladder.

He's swiftly grabbed this sponge, holds in his hands, and tears it apart. It's implicit that Spurt is pointing at Fang Yen: "Chen, give this to him! Mister Fang, you've to be on guard, hold on tight, don't miss what's going to happen next!"

The man looks puzzled: by touching thing, he doesn't feel this object weights a lot, quite the reverse, it's seen as a spongy mass slightly has pressed upwards.

Chen takes sponge from Fang's hands, placed it back in the box; he then locked this metallic mass up in storage with a key; and left with this box.

It's perceived sound, when Spurt's clapped hands that are noisily conducted tests upon his instructions: "Fellows, pay attention! It's all about levitation!"

Later, enters a cat under Chen Jung's watch: as this animal suddenly is elevating to the ceiling it's airborne.

With a piercing meow this animal having tossed around the room, been scared. A cat rapidly flew out of the window, where overlooked the park, from above.

Meantime, among those guests Fang Yen is obviously finding the situation paradoxical. Instinctively he's walked to the window, where seen a cat is descending: following this animal begun landing, down on the grass.

And yet, Spurt's tried to stop him: "Don't go to the window, Fang Yen!"

Chen meanwhile, rapidly delivered this cat to the garden, whereabouts a planted tree nurtured. On the spot he began calling for: "Minty! Minty! Doggy, the cat is in here! Look, everyone, the cat flew away!"

Right this moment a dog Minty raised its voice, and begun running up to the tree. Once the animal sees a cat, it starts barking, and has made a leap; heard this dog with a plaintive squeal; when it's suddenly elevated, and flying into the sky.

Ascending to the sky, Minty is kept barking, while dog size flown; still squeals, which could be heard across. This dog bark then, began fainting away. Spurt's assistant in a difficult situation, is calling this dog: "Minty! Minty! Come down! Good doggy, come to me!"

Saw this dog, in a flash does fly higher up to sixty feet in the air. Shortly after this animal began descending.

A dog was lastly discovered, when landed near Chen Jung. Seen animal's tumbled harshly on the turf, though it's being virtually dead. Providentially doctor's assistant has picked it up, and carried this dog towards meadow.

On the spot Chen Jung has resuscitated this dog that being close to fatal. Luckily, the animal survived; and is begun jumping with joy, like nothing have happened earlier.

Meanwhile, in laboratory Spurt is happily explaining to those guests: "Now, for the final experiment in our agenda!"

A Chinese man in his turn ignores Spurt; when he began walking towards the exit. Yet Spurt turns to face Fang Yen, looks at him, but he seems isn't content: "Honorable guests, wait a bit more!"

Spurt spins back; and deals promptly with his assistant, is instructing him: "Chen Jung, put on track a mass toad and turtle, then gently push away both these organisms with your foot!"

In all probability it's paradox: this toad jumped up is aerial, resulting it's flown over the bushes, trees, elevating higher and higher into the sky. Following slowly moved a turtle; like a toad sudden it's elevated - the animal is flying.

Fang alongside other guests have lost sight of a toad and turtle; and he kept watching the sky. Amazingly soon, a turtle is plunged on the ground.

Spurt to suave perplexity, is challenging this Chinese man: "What's your opinion on that, Mr. Fang? You still not convinced on my experiment of levitation?"

Fang's looked, as if been confused, whilst he's tongue-tied up: "I'm ohm… ohm…"- The Chinese man is fascinated, but uncertain, what he witnessed in this laboratory.

Foolishly one of the female guests said rather strange: "Excuse me, doctor, why did bring this toad? Is your assistance going to cook it? I love French cuisine!"

But Spurt disrupts her: "Madam, are you crazy? You're in a wrong place! This is not a fucking restaurant! Pardon my French; Madame at Monsieur, its camoufler! Madam, if you not stupid, you can see this is a bloody Laboratory in a Hospital!"

By quirk of fate, he was in doubt of apparatus that have appeared in front of his and other guest's eyes.

Instinctively, Fang proclaimed: "It's like I've swallowed a pill, predominantly a bitter one? Obviously it's paradox, what have occurred inhere?"

Spurt worked nonstop for over two hours, has conducted experiment after experiment, in this laboratory.

Finally another guest is having a word to say: "Doctor Spurt, what we saw, it were extraordinary! And you deserve to be called a genius! Bravo!"

Spurt has composed; then turns around: to prove one and for all that medical research succeeded, doctor calls on his assistant; is schmoozing:

"Chen Jung, you've to extend into more analyses?" He revolves, is facing those guests; and begun explaining of his experiments to everyone, to impress them: "All of you saw a metallic mass with microscopically thin walls, of desirable cavities, which were earlier filled with hydrogen. I'm declaring: I was successful in achieving the first flying ultra-light metal!"

Spurt halts talking; and has pointed to a group to keep quiet; in-between he is taken a deep breath. Almost immediately he is ongoing with explanation of search, making his case clear for those guests: "As for insects you saw in my experiments, these for instance, have the ability to descend on the spiders cobwebs. To be more specific, I've closed the insect's ducts glands,"- he halts talking; by taken a breath; he prolongs: "Sorry, I can't say more, for I've discovered, for the reason that I hate for someone to steal my ideas? Every bit of experiments that you witnessed here, I hope, can be characterized as levitation!" Spurt became silent for a minute; his look can be translated as delight. Then he's stating: "Now, can you all imagine, what a revelation would that be for transport equipment, and for the future constructions? All of you visualize, Skyscrapers could leave the Stratosphere, and are headed for the Flying Cities, somewhere in Space? Even settle in Milky Way or Mars?"

Recklessly Spurt starts walking to a cabinet, loaded with medications. Yet he's challenging, and is explaining to those guests his experiments:

"No one ever saw analogous that you witnessed with a cat, which is not a bird on wings, and it doesn't know how to fly? Yet, the animals or insects are well-preserved with its dispositions, which is necessary to flying!" Its become visible Spurt's expression read of be proud: "I hope you've all paid attention to animals behavior that I've shown to you? If you didn't, I must remind you that, in my first experiment, mister Fang Yen, I went in your area Physics of thin films." Spurt's kept writing on white-board, in tandem is clarifying for the guests: "I'd like you all pay attention to fundamental part of my experiments, which you'll appreciate that I took advantage of animals' instincts! For we in the lab have used of organisms full ability to make them levitate! You still don't believe me? A dog, for instance can jump, and we know that! All of you're surprised seen unpredictably as this dog Minty, elevated, though it's become scared, when flown. But this animal has almost got smashed, you all heard when my assistant ordered Minty to return?" Spurt goes silent; and turns to observe those guests.

Succeeding in getting people's attention, he raises hands, and revolves his palms over; is trying to reassure them, he tells more: "All of you saw a toad, which was being on very low level among other organisms' development. During my third experiment, this creature has died, before reaching cold of oxygen-poor air layers,"- he halts of talking; is taken deep breaths. Saw his shoulders have moved up and down, as if he's struggling for oxygen.

Spurt stood silently for a minute. To conclude, he's revealed: "You've watched Experiments conducted by me that proved with death the organisms would have disappeared.

'Every part of the organisms was indebted to fragmentation of the artificial radioactive elements, which would occur in the internal bodies of any animals or insects. And yet, the animals have the ability to fly! You all may think it's controversial? Their ability of levitation only disappears, be caused after internal body in organisms, would have collapsed or it could be fatal with the use of artificial radioactive elements..."

Spurt takes advantage of recess; is kept explaining to the guests: 'Now comes the conclusion: all these experiments were about levitation. Every part of this can be used widely, for instance: the more developed an animal with a higher nerve system is. Like dogs, the greater could be the result. In saying all this, Mastery of levitation is possible only with humans. And I'll become rich for my discovery! Let's use China for its phenomena, and for my success!'

Chapter 7

LONG time had passed. Some days, in Tibet's hospital ward appear Fiend and Evildoer having conversation with Spurt, and gesticulated, while the doctor begun nodding. Resulting doctor's taken out a set of pink pills from med-cabinet metal draw. As an endorsement Fiend slapped Song Chuan over his tiny shoulder; next he's ordering him: "Hey, you, boy, take the pills, and swallow it! You'll not go outside, unless you take these! It's for your own good, child!"

Time-in-between, Song Chuan's silent, then mechanically he bends his head to look at the wristwatch. Even if this boy is worried, resulting he quickly puts two pills in his mouth, and swallows them. Follow-on, effect of the pills due to its taste has taken its toll. Soon it's affected him: Song Chuan is begun feeling abnormal.

The next morning it's developed a crack of dawn, outskirts of Tibet Monastery: from a window are seen shadows of tree leaves, but up in blue-sky stars vanished. Tossing bats. It's a frosty night in Chinese provinces, because of winter season.

At the same day, by nighttime, this boy, starts telling Aaron his life story: 'My parents named me Song Chuan, since we were originally from the West China. My mom married my dad, when she wasn't even seventeen years.

'But my mom had died given birth to me, then my father was killed... So I grew up without be loved and cared by parents. First I began working in a Coalmine...'

Intuitively Aaron became sympathetic to this boy's tough life, and wished to know more: "Song Chuan, how did you end up in Coalmine?"

This boy bends his head, as if his spirits was in sorrow; and tells more: "You see, after my mother and father were dead, I became an orphan, since I haven't got brothers, or a sister to taken care of me,"- he halts of talking; whilst tears appear in his eyes. He is breathless too. The boy wipes tears with his elbow, and is ongoing with his story: 'Later I was taken by the High Govern, and placed working in the Coalmine. Working in Coalmine, I saw other orphans, like me, where they were starving..." The boy stops talking, saw his body trembled, he's sobbing.

'As you can see, I've survived!' The boy become speechless; by taken a heavy breath, he's ongoing:

"Due to my weak health, they moved me to a factory, where I worked from 8 am - until 6 o'clock, at night."

Hearing of boy's heartbreaking story, Aaron is distressed; and interrupted him: "Tell me, how did you come about to that Monastery?"

This boy takes a profound breath. Sorrow is seen in his eyes, when he prolongs with his life story: "Due to starvation, I was born weak, and wasn't given many years to live, by the doctors. Caused by my fragile health, I couldn't perform as good on labor, as those strong children." He became silence for a moment. By taken deep breaths, Song Chuan tells what be a shock to Aaron:

"Since I belonged to manual labor family, and poorly paid Chinese people, I've found myself in a situation, when my parents were dead, and there was no one to help, or support me financially," the boy's eyes promptly filled with tears.

As he's taken a deep breath, and began whispering: "Later, someone grabbed me, and had placed me in the care of Master Wong Da," Aaron knew this happens be Fiend.

"Now, as can you see the situation for me become dangerous, brother Bo." After he stops talking; and looks in Aaron's eyes, as if is begging for compassion.

Day-after-day be followed in Tibet. Once it's developed on the verge of midnight, and climate advanced into a spring.

Here's seen a full moon excel outwardly, in the atmosphere. Sky developed into lilac; seen space was sparking full of stars. Supervening some shooting stars would slowly plummet down.

One of the nights, Aaron discussed quietly with Song Chuan, while tells this boy to pretend, to keep up the charade; and he's talking with an expression of false-happiness.

All of sudden Aaron is begun hearing sneaky steps, and his expression changed to grim; yet he's whispered: "This is perhaps Evildoer or Fiend, coming from the corridor?"

Be in a difficult situation, Aaron stepped away from Song Chuan; and on the spot he starts discipline this boy, in a loud voice: "You've to read the 'Ancient Holy Books' of Guru Buddha that trusted to you, or you'll be punished!"

This boy seats in silence, seen his face has been blushing, primarily from a fever.

Meanwhile, Evildoer entered the room; Fiend is following him, both curious as always, seen Dens left the door open.

They've stopped, and both been watching this boy. It seems Aaron is thoughtful. Carelessly he's disturbed by Fiend's voice: "Son of Buddha! Spare no effort to work let me remind you: the Monks and I've helped you to grow. Today come the time, you've to teach by providence the youngsters and yourself, to become a proper Monk? If your mission to become Spiritual Leader of Buddha: 'It's time for your harvesting', as people say! Then go to work: you must serve those, who have educated and fed you, thank them for their care, and given you a shelter! You've the Highest Honor to dedicate yourself to Buddha services! I hope you're convinced with my reasons?"

During Dens pompous tone of speech, Aaron looked directly into his eyes, like a man with nothing to hide, but he was pretending.

Meanwhile, the boy's expression hasn't shown the slightest emotion, of what his soul neither reflected; nor a single muscle moved within it.

He lowered his eyes; and tried not to breathe, so as not to get attention from both horrible Fiend and Evildoer towards him.

Aaron in a difficult situation looks is thinking: "This boy has realized that his fate been decided? Now, his life comes to a turning point."

Aaron folds his palms together, as the Buddhists usually do, and 'took dust of their feet' of the 'Holy' Master. Ensuing he's bent over, touched with his hand Brian's feet, and with the same hand is swept fast his forehead. He's faking, while is talking: "My thoughts, my desires, and my life belongs to you, Master!"

When Fiend finished search-examining Aaron, and was pleased with the results. For the first time in all these years of tuition, he stroked Aaron's head: touched lad's fingertips to his chin, and kissed them. Resulting Dens puts a wide smile, like a gift to Aaron: "Now come with me, Xian Wei. Your first step is moving on a new path of life!"

So Song Chuan was left alone, in a critical time, he covers his face with both hands, for he couldn't contain himself, and began crying awfully.

Meanwhile, Aaron is following Fiend, like a well-behaved dog.

Minutes later they've barged in hospital laboratory, where appears Evildoer is seated near Dr. Hui Wei. There's seen a Chinese man, in the age of his twenties. Brian without delay began explaining: "Xian Wei, we brought you here to see Dr. Hui Wei, who is a scientist. He's famous having a reputation as a genius, in the field of surgery procedures.

His real name is Spurt, and you both can talk in English! So, behave well!"

"Master Guru, why I need to be examined by Dr. Hui Wei? I'm healthy!" Asked worriedly Aaron.

"Don't be difficult, Aaron, it's for your own good!" Be Brian reaction.

The next day, even if it's a sunrise, darkness still was visible outside. When Fiend entered a hospital ward saw Aaron's following. Dens is focused on him only; he then looks Aaron in the eyes, and instructed him: "Now, Xian Wei, the doctor need to run a few tests on you, including blood test. You haven't eaten breakfast, yet?" Inquired Fiend.

"No, second Master Guru!" Replied Aaron, seems be troubled.

"Xian Wei, remember to collect new clothes from housekeeper by tomorrow!" A Fiend delay of talking; and is observing Aaron from top to toe.

Though keeping in mind malicious thoughts, Fiend reveals: "Oh, I forgot to tell my boy, tomorrow, five-thirty in the morning, I shall pick you up personally, from your chamber. You heard what our doctor has instructed you? Not to eat, or drink! It's essential that you wash yourself thoroughly, and after wear on new clothing! Just be ready for me to pick you up!"

Aaron, in his turn submissively, bowed his head, still be nervous. Suddenly Evildoer gets up of his seat; is heading for the door. Before opening the door, he looks at the boy, then asked Aaron called Xian Wei: "How is Song Chuan doing?"

In hearing this, Aaron's vexed, and is reacting without hesitation: "A poor possession of concentration, by this schoolboy! I hope he'll improve."

Evildoer shakes his head, has responded: "Xian Wei, as Buddha said - Hope for the best. Prepare for the worst. And expect nothing."

On a whim Fiend has intruded, and lurched of Aaron's scowl that appears on his facial expression.

Dens reacted, with annoyance: "Because Song Chuan's disadvantaged in learning, he should get tougher punishment!"

At the same day, by dusk, Aaron has left the laboratory, Spurt called Dr. Hui Wei, indicated to Fiend and Evildoer: "Life itself is a miracle, fellows! My associate has clued-up us to a man, who will be the next Flying man?" He stops talking. As sign of a good deal, Spurt's nodded his head; but remains stern.

Later that day, on the brink of midnight, what a joy it is for Song Chuan, as he's felt a familiar hand patted his head. The boy asks directly: "Brother Bo, is it you?" Aaron slightly shakes this boy, to wake him up; instantly he began whispering into this boy's ear: "Yes, Song Chuan, it's me! Are you asleep?"

Without loosing a second, a boy gets up of his bed happily, but he's careful, thus is whispering: "No, bother Bo! I'm glad you back! Though, I was scared that might not see you again?"

Aaron's placed a smile; he's reaction by gladness, but in half-whisper: "Song Chuan, I'm back, don't be scared!"

Song Chuan interrupts Aaron, his head turns towards right; he looks as if is lost; but seems be concerned for Aaron's safety: "Why you're so long there? What they've wanted from you, brother Bo?"

Aaron's tongue-tied, as he switched attention to someone's steps behind the door. He has sensed risk; and inclines his head toward the door.

Seen Aaron's left eye blinked, and he is whispering to this boy: "Quiet! It's the Master... You know, he isn't Chinese, but an Englishman. His real name is Dens Fiend!"

Song Chuan nods; and cuts his wording: "I knew long before that Master wasn't a Chinese. And what did this doctor?"

Shortly, those footsteps have waded away. Aaron now became relaxed; sudden he has flashback of memories: "There is Dr. Hui Wei, and Wong Da! I heard Master exclaimed - It's me! Then Dr. Hui Wei, said - Fiend, why the hell, you come in here? Promptly Master Wong Da became angry. He blinked, Dr. Hui Wei then has corrected himself, saying 'Good evening, Master Wong Da! Did you bring Xian Wei? - Next he has called on Chen Jung, hurry up! Later Dr. Hui Wei has examined me, and said - It's healthy, and quite fit! In a few days we'll have him ready. - I saw Evildoer grimaced, and has commanded me: Xian Wei, come back here at dawn, before having breakfast! Most importantly, follow my instructions don't eat, take a bath, wash your body well, and put on new clothing. When I asked conventional clothing? He said 'No, hospital robes! That's all, it's complicated for you'?"

This boy interrupts Aaron, his head turns towards right; he looks as if is confused: "What all that means? What they intent to do with you?"

Aaron began patting his head: "They kept me long, but don't worry!" He halts talking; looks content; and gave a sneer. Impulsively, his face turns sad:

"Master kept me in facility, and he gave instructions - 'Obedience, obedience and more obedience!' But here you and I lie through our teeth, at every turn."

Aaron's expression altered to content: "Song Chuan, let's talk about something else? What Xian Wei means in Mandarin?"

This boy grins, angles his head; is responded: "The name Xian means 'flying', and Wei translates 'high'. But I like to call you Bo, it's significant, and translates as an elder brother!"

A sudden flashback of memories have flooded Aaron's mind, from the time when he was a child.

Almost immediately, Song Chuan brings him back to reality: "Brother Bo, are you well? What's wrong with you?"

Aaron is chuckling, begun whispering: "Don't worry, Song Chuan, I'm fine!"

And yet, Aaron wouldn't tell this boy, what he heard Fiend decided about Yuan Lu's fate; once he has described this little girl's upbringing: "An Englishman, like many others had conquered Yuan Lu's mother in China… We were aware all those years ago that her mother was one of the singers and dancers in a Strip club. Evildoer, don't be a pain in the ass we haven't lost many lives?

'We could gain from the situation, because the inhabitants had suffered in the hands of those Monks!"

Something has sunk to Evildoer, and he's endorsed Fiend "In that case, what we should do with this girl, Yuan Lu'?"

Aaron's kept recalling everything they've said: "Fiend angles his head; and puts in a picture some sort of future that awaits on her, the same what we did to others, make her vanish! Who will look for a busted, poor little girl, like Yuan Lu?" These words have stuck in Aaron's mind.

Chapter 8

THE next day, at crack of dawn, Aaron bears over charade; with this mood he went to the hospital's facility, having a strategy of his own, how to behave.

Once Aaron has arrived in laboratory, where he's met Spurt, who's wearing a blue robe, fitted with a matched color cap that's concealed his hair.

Twenty minutes later Aaron with other nurses have entered hospital ward, which reminiscent of an operating theater.

Making next stop of their walk is the X-ray room, in which a more complex of the unusual equipment seen that have been installed in there. On the spot Spurt orders him walking to an odd looking apparatus: "Now, young man, go pronto over behind the screen, because you need to undress yourself. And leave your cloth there! Next, lie down on this table, under apparatuses, where you'll be lined with white oilcloth."

As always, Aaron obeyed, and is nodding his head. Be in an extreme difficult situation, he thought: "In case, if the doctor suggest that I've to go deep into hypnotic dream? I'm quite capable to simulate it, with inspiration ally." Except, Aaron has underestimated because this be a critical moment.

Soon after, Spurt or Dr. Hui Wei, is ordered Aaron: "Xian Wei, swallow this white powder that be diluted in water!"

Be motivated Spurt rotated, has commanded his assistant: "Chen Jung, bring the mask in here, please?"

His assistant underway is in motion, to the adjacent room: "Yes, Dr. Hui Wei!"

Minutes later assistant returned, is wearing a similar blue robe with a blue cap that covers his head, and carrying a mask aimed for surgery procedure. These rest of staffs nearby are too wearing identical blue hospital robes.

Without delay Spurt bends over Aaron's face wore a white mask, off this came a strong sugary smell. Spurt ordered Aaron: "Breathe deeply, Xian Wei! And now start counting aloud, to a hundred! Deal?"

"Okay, doctor! I'm counting: one ... Two ... Three..." Calculating Aaron.

After a few minutes, Aaron's speech altered, become a faint voice. By the end of the second ten, he is adrift from counting to halt. It's caused Aaron loosing consciousness.

It's approached the end of the day, waking up in hospital facilities; Aaron doesn't recognize the place, which has inducted earlier. As his eyes get open, the image has been unclear for him, at first. Despite Aaron's blur vision, his mind is active: "Whatever they did to me?" He's begun observing facilities, which obscured with curtains.

Hearing voices, once Aaron's newly regained consciousness it's scared him; and slowly, but surely, he opens his eyes and absorbing. The first person he saw standing over him is Spurt, talking to someone: "The procedure went well! That's all I can say."

Aaron disoriented; despite feeling weak and having a faint voice, he begun talking: "I feel sick, my head is buzzing! Doctor, what's wrong with me?" On the spot Aaron slowly bows head, and noticed that he is laid on a stretching bed; down on the floor in hospital's office-lab. The condition seems be made him chaotic: "Dr. Hui Wei, I've a bad feeling in my mouth? Why is that?"

Spurt appears with a smile; is speaking gently: "Well, Xian Wei! You said you've a bad feeling in your mouth? Don't you worry about that, my boy! It'll pass. Lie down quietly, and don't talk! Just relax."

Aaron, for the time being, has obeyed doctor's instruction, still laid on stretch-bed, half-dressed; unusual with red from betel lips, like smoked a pipe, and is fanning to himself.

Evildoer appears from nowhere, extends of talking: "Soon you must pack your stuff, Xian Wei, as we'll embark you into Space!"

The circumstances that have occurred, made Aaron confused.

At some stage of Aaron transition from surgery to recovery, Evildoer alongside Fiend would come in his ward on regular basis.

Once upon a day, come into view Spurt walks halfway around the room to reach Evildoer; follow-on turns his eyes aside, is indicating at Aaron: "Evildoer, I'm warning you, remember be gentle with him!" Brian curtsies, as if is approved.

Spurt's assistant, Chen Jung too bends; and nods his head: "Yes, Dr. Hui Wei!"

During lunch-break Spurt, stood shaken from be in doubts: it seems he is mad, when reassessing surgery experiments that have been performed on Aaron. At the same time the whole thing has made Aaron disoriented.

PART – II
NO WINGS NEED TO FLY

Chapter 9

TWO days after the surgery procedure that has performed on Aaron, which did a doctor, kept him under observation. He is seen in hospital ward; when in a critical moment Spurt has decided: "We must prepare you, Xian Wei carefully for the role of the Flying man!"

The next day, in mid-morning, Spurt is seen composed, when opens up to Aaron; jointly he's articulating: "You a strong man, Xian Wei! Could you lift up another man of the same weight, as yourself?"

Although, life in Monastery had taught Aaron to be careful, crucially when he's resolved not to trust odd individuals.

Called Xian Wei, he's found all being thought-provoking; but reacted with care: "I've not tried yet, doctor! But if you think I could? Then I may…"

On a whim Spurt interrupts him: "Every strong person could lift weight, equal to his or her body weight, even more, remember that, my young friend!"

Afterwards this scientist turns aside; and ordered to the person who has appeared at his call: the assistant: "Chen Jung, please, come here, and keep Xian Wei safe!"

In a flash he turns to glance aside at those men; and is ongoing: "Now, Xian Wei, go ahead straighten your body, and do a single jump, as you sit in this chair!"

Seven days have passed, from the time when Aaron undergone surgery procedure.

One upon an evening at hospital's ward, Aaron is resting in bed, as usual. Surprisingly memories of his early childhood began flooding Aaron's mind. He instinctively was recalling of all horrors that he has suffered in here, whilst reflects on his past: "Horrors had caused me live in fear, and overshadowed my upbringing in the Monastery. It still lasts in my soul 'a few blades of grass and the sand in desert,' as Chinese folks would, say."

"Brilliant job, Xian Wei!" Spurt's randomly disturbed he's thoughts; then dramatically puts his thumb upfront: "At least for me! But not everyone, including Evildoer will be pleased, but that's his or her business. Well, you fell as an old say - Hurt to blame twine. Without it, however, you're risking to break your skull on the ceiling. Rotate, we'll strap you solid; but you don't know how to control your powers? Listen, and listen carefully, Xian Wei! Now let's get to business, you're capable to achieve what any human wouldn't be able to dream about. You can fly, my young friend! In order to fly, you only have to wish for it. Apart from climbing Alps, you'll be able to fly faster or slower, and make turns in any direction, to go down by will. It's crucial to control yourself, especially to manage your body well, when you fly. As you get up, sit down, or lie down. Do you understand all that happen to you?"

This situation is making Aaron bewildered, to what Spurt has indicated: "Doctor, I try to get use to this situation? However..."

Without losing a second, Spurt orders Aaron: "Well, young man, you need some time to adjust to it.

'Now, try to jump in another chair; and this time, don't pull the chair, only think about what's your demand, in order to fly?"

Aaron obeys the orders; and sat down in the chair, is laid back rational, kept talking: "How this works, doctor? Is it through control of my mind I can ascend, then descend?"

By quirk of fate, Aaron suddenly began slowly elevating to quite a height according to measures. Next surprisingly he's flown across the room. "It's for real? I'm flying!"

After he's started tumbling down; resulting is seated down in a chair near Spurt, who's stating: "I wouldn't believe it, if I've not seen a miracle myself! Congratulations, Xian Wei! You're making a speedy recovery, and progressing, my boy! Now, try without the chair!"

Aaron, in his turn is amazed, when nosily disrupted Spurt: "Without a chair? Doctor, do you think, I can actually fly without wings?"

Spurt began laughing, splashing red saliva: "Of course you can fly, Xian Wei! Ha-ha! You thought a chair was a plane, such as bashing witch? No way! From now on, you become the flying man. It's not higgledy-piggledy. You the first person ever, who can fly without wings or mechanisms, be proud of, my boy!" He halts talking; then Spurt began yelling: 'Lift up, Xian Wei!'

From a shock or after, Aaron has got up from his chair, and promptly elevates; and still remains in the air. Yet Spurt said: "Adventurer? Ha-ha-ha! Am I a charlatan, Xian Wei? No way!"

Spurt recalled his colleague in sciences, who haven't value him, contrary rejected some time ago similar tests: "They did not believe in me..."

Unexpectedly laboratory's door gets wide open, and on threshold stepped in Fiend and Fang Yen, in a way their shoulders saw shuffled frontward.

They're instantly noticed Aaron who has hung between floor and ceiling, and for a minute, opened theirs mouths wide, it seems one and all is petrified. Fang Yen, on the spot painfully bites his dry lips; then is begun bowing like a question mark.

There up Aaron spins effortlessly, suddenly is plunged. He then slowly starts elevating to the ceiling.

"Come on, fellows, don't you see a miracle now? What are you dumb heads?" Spurt saw an opportunity, and hailed those guests triumphantly.

Aaron meanwhile, reflexively sank to the floor.

Fang Yen came to his senses. A sudden stride to close the window, on the way he is half-whispering: "What a disregard on my part?"

Involuntarily he walked across to reach Aaron, with a twisting mouth and a smile; he's enthusiastic about: "It's better for your flying than walking, young man? Isn't it true?"

Fang Yen forced himself overcome envy; seems be amazed. And bows like is worshiping him, as uttering: "Spurt, colleague congratulations! You a genius!"

As a good will Spurt moves towards, raised his arm, began slapping Fang over his shoulder.

Time-in-between Fiend rushed to the phone, and called someone: "Evildoer, it's urgent! Come down to the laboratory in Spurt's ward!"

After Fiend rotates, and sees to Aaron; is asking him: "How did you feel when you flew over, Xian Wei?"

Aaron hasn't got over the heavy medication; he seems is in shock: "It was worthy? But I don't understand what's going on?" He stops talking; takes gulps of air; still is disoriented: "At first, it was cold and discomfort that went through my body. After the surgery I've experienced pain mostly in my bones and forelegs."

Fiend takes a chance, and is in smooth talking: "Xian Wei, you're lucky bastard! Your head stirred up? But the result is greater than we anticipated, your body consistently is reacting to remedy better than we expected before surgery?"

Aaron in his turn responded; yet he wasn't happy: "But I didn't agree to all that!"

On the spot Spurt's declaring: "Mental abilities, my young friend, must not be violated!"

"Um... Yeah, do you think so, doctor?" Asked Aaron called Xian Wei; still is feeling abnormal.

"Undoubtedly! Fortunately in your case the surgery went splendidly!"

The next day, Aaron's remained in hospital ward overnight, but been silent. He's taken heavy breath; and is begun thinking:

"Loneliness and a miserable childhood with cruelty I knew-how it was in my childhood. But those kids have no friends, no families to support them? It's like I was? Song Chuan is a poor kid, and already has found himself at risk, stepping only on the first stage of a ladder of torments.

If this boy could only manage, or he's to be relocated from such hell, cause he cannot retaliate, for he's a child?" Aaron is laid silently, observing the situation from a different angle.

Surprisingly rather a clue has struck him: "But I'm able to fly?"

In a difficult situation Aaron's self-control drove away his miserable thoughts. See his foot forthwith does steps firmly on the ground: "Now I know what to do."

Chapter 10

MANY days have passed since Aaron had a surgical procedure; and was already released from the hospital.

At this time of the year it's an extraordinary a vision of purple dusk with virtually bloodshot in the Skies, which well-lit open-air, despite of darkness. Since spring comes visiting this forgotten part of China, taken control from winter.

Right this moment Fiend entered Aaron's chamber, is focused on him only. Fiend hasn't come alone; following him is a stranger, who strides beside him, this happens is detective Greenwood.

Aaron, meanwhile, submissively bowed his head, as a sign of respect. From a shock or after, Andrew's look changed to stun; and he is thought: "It's him? Yes, Xian Wei is Aaron Dalton, Christina's brother? I've no doubt about! He looks exactly like the portrait of their parents. I'm finally in luck!"

Fiend suddenly gets up of his seat; is walking to the door. Before exiting, he looks at this boy; on the spot asked Aaron: "Xian Wei, how the student Song Chuan is learning? Any progress?"

Aaron contrary is wary, reacting without hesitation: 'No, second Master. This student, Song Chuan's still got a poor possession of concentration!'

Fiend jerked of the boy's scowled that shown upon his look; he then has given up.

Later on, when the night-developed; prior going to bed, be one foot on the threshold, Aaron without hesitation forced this boy to read; he is calm, strict and demanding: "Song Chuan, start reading passages from the Buddha's Holy books! Recite these aloud, and in a singing voice!"

Shortly close to midnight, when takes over changeably - the bell began ringing. Aaron turns on talking: 'Did you hear the bell rang? It's the hour for your bedtime, Song Chuan!'

This boy's gladly slammed a hardcover book. Aaron meantime, blew out the oil lamp. Seen both sat on a rug, shoulder-to-shoulder, in dark, and their tongue-tied.

An hour later those two were still seated down on a mat, in Yoga position, looking into blackness silently. As a repercussion, Aaron began whispering into boy's ear: "Song Chuan, listen carefully! Do you know another time Dr. Hui Wei to be called Dr. Spurt?"

This boy moved his neck up and down. Aaron's ongoing: "He's made me the flying man! You saw with your own eyes? Now, Song Chuan, you know my secret I can fly, like a bird!"

This boy is still bewildered, but not scared: "Where are your wings, brother Bo?"

When the boy asked him, he has seen that Aaron's shoulders fidgeted.

Aaron has made laughter, at the same time as responded: "I don't need wings, Song Chuan, since I'm able to fly without them. It's like we fly in our dreams,"- a sense of restrain has made Aaron shut up; and think by a pulsation.

He resumes of talking: "They want to show me to people as a miracle? But I want to fly away from this horrible place?" Aaron became silent for a minute; and is listening to some noises behind the walls.

After he is whispering in a sharp voice: "Look over there, can you see window is open?"

This boy nods, is getting ready to talk, as a repercussion Aaron interrupts him: "Shush."

Now both began hearing footsteps are echoing. Though Aaron placed a finger to his mouth, as if is cautious: "Shush! I heard footsteps."

This boy on the spot, whispered: "Yes, I do hear footsteps too."

Aaron cuts his word; then puts fingers to his mouth, as signal: "Don't speak."

Unforeseen, the front door has creaked; Fiend's voice been heard from behind the door: "Are you awake, Xian Wei?"

Aaron and the boy have felt Evildoer's influence too; when his voice from exterior of the door, yelled: "Xian Wei, can you hear, me?"

Aaron is dodging in it, and mumbled, as if pretending that is waking up: "Uh, ohm. Yes, second Master!"

Next Evildoer speaks-up: "Okay, Xian Wei, go back to sleep!"

Awhile later, the door gets half-open, when in the room has slipped a stranger, Aaron and the boy saw him earlier, he's head pocked through the door. This is Andrew; while Aaron and this boy watching him with shock.

On the spot Aaron alone speaks to him: "Sir, what are you doing here? You not supposed to be in this chamber! You get us in troubles, and we'll be locked up?"

It's Andrew's hand that covered Aaron's mouth: "Shush, I can hear footsteps."

Soon, Fiend's footsteps haven't been heard any longer. Those three were kept tongue-tied.

Ultimately Aaron breaks silence; is interrogating Andrew: "Who are you? What do you want?"

On a critical moment Andrew's listening to incoming noises; then whispered: "Don't fear me! I'm Andrew Greenwood! And I'm here to look for you. I'm on the request of Christina, your sister, who's tried to find you for a long time, but she couldn't…"

Be in Monastery over a decade; and have experienced hell; Aaron learned not to trust strangers easily.

On this instance Aaron's expressed his opinion, when in a sharp voice: "And how would I know, you're telling me the truth here?"

Seems the situation is challenging; Andrew promptly puts a hand in his pocket at upper body of his jacket; and takes out a picture, then shows to Aaron: "Look at this photo! There's the entire Dalton family; and that's your sister Christina! Now you convinced?"

Andrew couldn't convince him; it seems his effort is preposterous. Resulting Aaron is questioning: "You said, your name is Andrew Greenwood?"

Andrew in his turn nods his head, agreeably: "Yes! And I'm a private investigator. Your sister Christina hired me to find you.

"I can assure you that I'm not the enemy here! I know, due to greed and mutual agreement between London Lawyers, over a decade ago, Crofter took you in your childhood on a cruise. He brought you all the way to China, in this forsaken Institution! Aaron, let me help you? Tomorrow I'll talk to Evildoer and Fiend. After that, the two of us will leave this place for good."

Aaron interrupts him; alone has a word to say: "Oh God, no! Don't even think about talking to these awful men. They wouldn't let me leave alive." He stops talking. By taken a deep breath, he is stating: "You may not know, but I've the ability to fly? I plan to take Song Chuan you see here, with Yuan Lu, and we'll fly faraway from this horrible place!"

Andrew looks, as if be astonished; at the same time can't believe what he heard; and nervously laughed: "Well then, I'll help all of you're to escape!"

Chapter 11

~❦~

THE next day, when night reached peripheral, Aaron was seen in his chamber. Before going to bed, he has forced this boy to read. He's seemed been calm, strict and demanding: "Song Chuan, start reading a few passages from Buddha's 'Holy' books! Recite aloud, and sing!"

It seems from the boy's attention has not lost that Aaron is out of control; and he asked his loyal friend: "Why, did you keep looking in the window? What did you see in there, brother Bo?"

For a minute Aaron's expression was with shadow of concern; then he came to his senses: 'Trees in the park have rustled in the wind it foretells a rain. Listen, Song Chuan, do you hear from afar a thunder? Look, the sky is still bright, with the sparkling stellar. At the beginning of a formation of the Universe...'

This boy looks as if is lost; and he intruded: "Brother Bo, I don't understand what you just said? Because you're using such big words, I cannot follow you?"

Aaron puts a smile; and began patting his hair: "I know you don't, Song Chuan! But look at the sky, there's the right side of pale hazy band in the Milky Way. And when the dark clouds approaching, it's an amazing view!"

Soon after both perceived din its rustle of the first big drops of rain. Now Aaron's sighed with a breath of relief.

At this moment by crushing darkness, a melodic Bell awakes, and began ringing. Aaron meanwhile, listens to noises for a tick; then he attends to: "Now the Bell rang. It's time for you go to bed, Song Chuan!"

The boy slammed a thick book. Aaron blew out the lamp. The boy hesitated, but asked Aaron anyway: "Brother Bo, can I stay a bit more? I'm not tired!"

They both sat on a mat shoulder-to-shoulder, in darkness, but silent. It came as a shock once Song Chuan feels Aaron has elevated him, ensuing he stood behind the boy's back. Aaron has clenched Song Chuan close to him, and elevated to the ceiling. On the spot he kept holding him; and whispered into boy's ear, with a soft laughter: "What lightweight you are?"

The boy looks be confused, but asked Aaron anyway: "Brother Bo, what those words mean, you've said?"

Aaron is whispering: "I meant to say you aren't heavy. Song Chuan, would you like me to lift you up even higher?"

The boy has sensed that Aaron raised him to the ceiling by, which his small head touched the top. He held him up; all is made Song Chuan panicky: "Brother Bo, do you really have such long arms? I'm scared, what are you God, or an Angel?"

Aaron grasps of boy's shock; and begun laughing; then he's whispered: "Don't be scared! I'm neither God, nor Angel! I'll get you down, Song Chuan!"

Extreme situation has made Aaron cautious; consequently he slowly descended; is kept holding this boy tight, until he touched down the ground.

Later, in chamber Aaron still wasn't asleep, being seated opposite to Song Chuan on the mat, in yoga position, both of their legs curved on the floor.

Sudden rotation, and Aaron seizes Chuan's wrist; and is whispering in the boy's ear: "Song Chuan, listen carefully, you know Dr. Hui Wei?"

This boy nods his head; but is kept silent. Aaron on the spot began explaining in a low voice: "He has made me the flying man! You saw with your own eyes? Picture this I can fly, like a bird!"

Song Chuan appears is stunned: "Where are your wings, brother Bo?" Asked this boy.

He unexpectedly sensed Aaron's shoulders fidgeted, when he is ongoing softly, but tolerantly: "You asked me about that before? I don't need wings, Song Chuan, because I can fly without them." He became quiet, thought for a tick. Next Aaron prolonged with his story: "They want to reveal me to the world as a miracle? But, I want to fly faraway from this horrible Monastery!"

Hearing of his decision breakout, the boy is begun crying: "What will become of me? It's so cruel inhere. I could die without your protection, Brother Bo!"

Aaron looks with concern in Chuan's eyes, be compassionate toward him: "Quiet! Don't cry! I'll take you with Yuan Lu, and we'll all fly-off! You a lightweight, and I could fly with you at my back?"

The boy's hands begun shaken: "Yes! Take me out of this Hell with you, please, brother Bo! Or I'll die in here!"

Aaron shushes him; alone listened what has occurred behind walls. Only then he is able to talk, but seemingly tense: "Can you hear the rustling of a rain? It's a good sign. In the darkness, no one can see us?"

He has frozen intuitively; by taken a deep breath he then turns aside to look in the window.

At last, he's begun whispering: "Did you leave the window open, Song Chuan?"

This boy bows his head, and is on the verge of saying... All of a sudden, those footsteps are heard reverberating. Aaron puts the right hand to his mouth: "Shush! I hear someone's walking."

Song Chuan on the spot is whispering: "Yes, I do hear footsteps too."

Aaron impulsively disrupts him; and alone is whispering: "Don't talk."

Rapidly, the front door creaked. Next a familiar voice to be heard from behind the door this is Fiend, who he is asking: "Are you awake, Xian Wei?"

Aaron and Song Chuan overheard again Fiend's sharp voice, coming from outside: "Xian Wei, are you there? Can you hear me?"

Aaron tries to make-believe it, as if he has just waked up; and in a faint voice: "Ohm... I'm sleeping, Master!"

When the door gets widely open, Fiend's head slipped into a half-open ingress; he then walks in the chamber. Aaron sat on bed makes-believe, and faked as if be stunned: "Oh, it's you, Second Master?"

Fiend began observing the room from side to side, as if he's mistrusted him: "Why don't you shut the window down, Xian Wei? I can see bath of water on the floor, coming from the rain!" Fiend, so-called Master of Buddha, points to a windowsill. Once he's approached the window; and closed it with a thud, all together he's lowered the blinds. Aaron by now has realized that Fiend was spying on him.

After Fiend has left, Aaron is deeply thinking: "Fiend doesn't trust me? The window can be opened, what if they set watchmen outside my hole-in-the-wall? It's crucial to raise the curtain, and start the alarm?"

Following, by midnight, Song Chuan is seated on a mat, shivering like a leaf; it seems he's being with a fever. Motivation forced him having a word to say; though he's whispered cautiously: "Clap of a thunder sounded somewhere close, and have repeated powerfully. I'm scared, brother Bo!"

Aaron in his turn tries to cheer him up: "Don't be scared, little brother! Do you see in the sky flashes of lightning lit up? It's a good sign. In the darkness, no one will see us." He clams up, as if be vigilant. Next he rotates, and looks in the window: "And the curtain in our room fell on a blue flame from its glow. You will not lose me! And you will go with Andrew tomorrow, then we all meet again! Decided?"

The next night was decisive for that quartet on escaping. It's past after two o'clock in the morning, when Aaron entered Yuan Lu's chamber. He began wakening this girl up, and is whispering: "Yuan Lu, it's time to wake up!"

Randomly heard rain outside swooshed the wind, because of the storm is looming. It's unforeseen: Aaron walks to the window, where on lintel with a frowning face duplicated. Yuan Lu brushed her teeth, and washed her face; after is dressed up.

An hour later, Aaron and this girl were kept in chamber. Once Aaron raised his arm, and takes a wooden peg on the wall, then is whispering into a towel strait to girl's ear: "Yuan Lu, let's go outside together!"

Its mysterious, girl's out of curiosity: "Brother Bo, where you're taken me?"

Aaron's indicating up on the ceiling.

As those two lifted a square like wing, access is led to extra room that remained empty. Without delay, they're silently have slipped out in the corridor.

Yuan Lu is following him, as they take en route: "It's completely dark down here? I don't know where we've to go, brother Bo?"

Aaron went ahead, has led Yuan Lu, who's clutching safely, with a rope to him on its end like chain that is knotted. This way she is following him. Meanwhile, all around remained silent, because everyone was asleep.

A minute ago Aaron and Yuan Lu have ascent, then went down the stairs; before they silently vanished in a long corridor...

Shortly they're begun climbing steep wooden staircases, covered with old carpet. Both are walking quietly across another corridor; when Aaron suddenly ordered Yuan Lu: "Stay behind me!"

Once they've reached access, Aaron thrown a hatch that is leading to the rooftop. Walking in outside it's already arisen dawn in this part of Chinese Tibet, where still seen darkness in the air.

Though a few steps away was a poor vision on this facility, due to a mist, which has covered the entire Sky.

It's still early morning; half-hour later arrived Andrew in a cab, this he hired earlier; seen the car stopped nearby Monastery's entry. He gave instructions to the driver: "Wait for me, for I'm bringing someone. And both of us have to be taken to the airport!"

At some stage of their getaway, alfresco lightning was visible; it's blinded up Aaron and this girl in a flash. Following both heard thunder; it seems the rain has soaked.

Without losing time, those two climbed on flat rooftop, and have stood there, even if thunder struck. Aaron and Yuan Lu haven't got much time to think of danger they're facing. And on the spot both accepted wisdom of life, on the go, to survive: since they've nothing to lose, only to gain.

On a critical point, Aaron bends down; and commands to this girl: "Climb up on my back, Yuan Lu!"

Sees the girl has obeyed him, whilst bends her head: "Yes, brother Bo, at once!"

After Yuan Lu has climbed at his back, in order to seat her steady behind; Aaron's resulting is knotted the girl up around his waist effectively with ropes.

To validate he turns head to see if the girl's tied solid or maintained proper, and comfortable. Aaron looks around for the safety reason, simultaneously is thinking.

Though he's grumpy: "Thanks to flashes of lightning, I can see Monastery's courtyard full of water? I glimpsed it's sparked like a Lake. For all those years the Monastery's wall have triggered my friends and me with fear on being there. It's more like been some thought of Institute of horrors."

Chapter 12

THE next morning, locals witnessed Aaron is flying; at his spinal be seated this girl, while she's clung to him.

Flying Aaron's found himself at vulnerability; and he spoke to: "Yuan Lu, I'll take you down over the fence, cause I've to return, and make sure Song Chuan wasn't left behind? I might bring him along? Then we'll fly as far as possible so that no-one catches us."

The girl nods her small head, as if is conforming: "Yes, we must do it, bother Bo!"

Finding themselves in an extreme danger, both brave broods are having made a decision in midair.

Later, in the afternoon, Aaron is seen airborne, but his whole body covered with sweat, and he's gasped for air: "We must fly far way from the horrible Monastery. Thank God, for the storm that He sent us, but it has passed. Now rain subsided. However, the wind is blowing strongly."

In an extreme situation Aaron began breathing profoundly; and decided: "At least we must reach the Pacific Ocean? Although, down there we can die?" He called Xian Wei, has strained his last strength.

Seen this girl's clung to him, and he felt she's frigid at his back, as if is having high temperature that resulted from a fever.

In a life-threatening situation Aaron became worried about girl's health: "Yuan Lu, are you sick?"

She pats over Aaron's shoulder, but is concern: "Possibly! But, don't worry about me brother, Bo! Keep flying!"

Aaron in his turn is logical: "I'll safe her, whatever the cost is! We'd fly in storms and dark, to unknown destiny for us it's crucial surviving!"

The next day, has developed an amethyst crack of dawn, it's an opportunity for Aaron and the girl flying to Tianjin, located: on 'Bohai Gulf', in Northeast borders of Chinese mainland.

Hours later, Aaron come within reach of the Pacific Ocean; and flew over, there seen they've been caught in the middle of sea waves.

Another day of flying for Aaron has improved; when suddenly from nowhere the girl is begun hearing noises: before her eyes - have appeared an airplane raised.

By quirk of fate Aaron too heard a giant bumblebee buzzing behind. Turning his head, he saw an airplane approaching straight at him, and is flying low-slung, but not fast-moving.

Yuan Lu's sensed risk, and tells Aaron: "Brother Bo, behind me is a huge bird!"

Suddenly Aaron began laughing freely: "Girl, it's not a bird, this's an airplane! And we'll fly with this, possible on its rooftop?"

Although, Yuan Lu's got uncertainties: "How?"

Aaron slants his head towards the aircraft: "You'll see. But you need all your strength to hold on to its edging, Yuan Lu!"

Sensing danger that be resulted from extreme situation, an aircraft began rapidly plummeting; and on the way lost its speed.

Aaron's become concerned; on the spot, thinking: "Maybe it's a pursuit after me and the kids?"

He still is flying, speculating; when seen the airplane has already flown in close proximity to him.

Although he was in midair, and about a stone fall down to the ground, but in a difficult situation in deliberation, he's definite: "Fiend couldn't chase me on the airplane? What if I to be caught airborne? 'And their search advance to the extent that in aircraft is faster to catch me? What if the police start shooting from this plane? No, it's false alarm!"

Remaining in the air, the pilot from the aircraft could not help, but spotting Aaron is airborne, with a little girl that be seated at his back. And all that has happened in midair, during an airlift.

Instinctively Aaron decided: "I'll rise above the aircraft, and clutch on under its structure together with Yuan Lu?"

At some stage of airborne, came a critical point: when he's decided: "Yes, I'll rise above the plane, and skip under its wings. This way we could fly towards other places in China, and faraway from that awful Monastery!"

The moment, an airplane pilot has passed right below them; from a shock or after Yuan Lu began shouting: "Yes! Let's descend on plane's wings, Brother Bo?"

While this duo flew in close proximity to the airplane. On a whim both of the humans are having clung to structure's wing. Swiftly, those two have stuck to plane's right section, during the entire flight.

Eventually the plane slowly began gaining speed, and it's raised up to the Sky.

Aaron finds the situation amusing, and chuckles: "Traveling like this on airplane wing, is a lot of fun! Isn't it true, Yuan Lu?"

This girl's agreed, and shakes her head, kept holding tight to his back and head. By way of relaxing, she's stuck out her tongue to sniff. Aaron has felt her move; his foot smacks her haunch; and he orders her in a serious voice: "Don't do this again, it's hard enough to carry you at my back, Yuan Lu! Understood?"

Suddenly Yuan Lu began shouting with joy: "Brother, I can see through the window people in that plane, above us! In there are sitting Song Chuan and mister Andrew!"

Aaron raises his head, saw at first glance those two who are placed rear of the airplane, by a window-plane: "You right, girl! I can see them on the plane too!"

Both humans are having clung firmly to the plain's titanium surface, for period of time.

It's passed many hours. Minutes ago dusk have covered the sky with lilac shade that made frigid.

Meanwhile, on the plane appears a peculiar Caucasian male this is Andrew. Next to him be seated Song Chuan, who's seen close to glass-sill of the aircraft.

At this moment, observed Aaron and this girl is adjusted to plane's rooftop for many hours; and flying farthest from Tibet, en route to Guangzhou, with location of the Pearl River Delta, in Southeast China.

Hours later Aaron and Yuan Lu left plane's rooftop; since they've decided flying to anew destination.

Time-in-between after a long flight, the plane landed late at night: when have reached its destination.

Presently, Andrew and Song Chuan were having arrived in Guangzhou Airport, where seen the travelers disembarked, and where along with others, are noticed this duo adjoining.

The next day, Aaron has flown of time-consuming; an airlift caused him feeling eventually tired, whilst is too carrying Yuan Lu upon his spinal.

PART – III
"SKY LORD"

Chapter 13

MANY days have passed, since those four fled the Monastery. In mid-morning Aaron was flying far-reaching; sudden noises he and Yuan Lu began hearing coming to the sky.

Looking down, Aaron and the girl's eyes are spotting a ship below, navigating the River. He's instantly sensed danger in that extreme situation; surprisingly a savior idea came to his mind: "Spot on!"

On the spot he speaks to: "Yuan Lu, lets get down, to catch this vessel? What do you think? Should we take a risk?"

This girl puts a smile for him; gladly nods her head: "Yes, brother Bo, let us descend on the ship's roof, at once!"

By nighttime, Aaron and Yuan Lu have landed long ago on the ferry. They've settled on boat's roof, where both sat, for seven hours.

Unforeseen: they're begun hearing noises; following screams coming from one of cubicles, down stairs. Expression on Yuan Lu has altered its read: she became scared; though is asking: "Brother Bo, what is going on downstairs?"

Aaron gets up, walks to observe, be frank: "I don't know, but we've to keep quiet. Don't get people's attention towards us both, girl!"

Briefly, down in ship's cubicle, boxes that have been brought earlier, and placed there, were packed with Chinese currency. It was a planned robbery, and has taken place on a boat, at midnight by some unidentified persons.

Time-in-between, those thieves have been making a tricky escape, taken with them stash of cash, via almost a three square foot hole, in vessel's roof.

Meanwhile, Aaron and Yuan Lu have felt danger been looming; and they frozen as from a shock or after: when eyewitness the thieves are making their escape through ship's rooftop. Lucky for this duo, those robbers haven't seen them both, up on rooftop; otherwise who knows what might happen to them?

It currently seems night was coming to an end. Yuan Lu sat alongside Aaron on boat's rooftop that navigating all the way to Guangzhou (or Canton); this is not far from Hong Kong.

Aaron hasn't snoozed; and before dawn, seen him been up and about. After he instructs Yuan Lu as they're in the midst of turmoil: "Let's glide on, and takeoff from rooftop, or we'll be caught! Climb on my back, Yuan Lu, and hold-on tight!"

On a critical point this girl picks up ropes, climbs on Aaron's back; and he's secured her there.

"Okay, I'll do that, brother Bo!" Despite the girl trusted him, it seems her be unhappy that Aaron wasn't an Angel.

Without delay, Aaron elevates with Yuan Lu, who sat at his spinal.

The next day, in the early hours of morning, the vessel crossed 200 miles (or 321 kilometers), and had disembarked at Chinese port of Guangzhou.

When the vessel pulled into the Port, it has a person-sized a hole in roof, in one of its compartment.

Soon, the news broadcast: 'Overnight it was a robbery on Chinese ferry that crossing...' Locals believed rumors: Flying man did the robbery. Those thieves actually have made escape with an enormous stash of cash, stolen through 2, 5 square foot hole, on the ferry's roof.

The police Chief beside the staff were seated near where guarded, and thinking: "How to avoid scandals?"

On the boat remained masses of boxes, packed with millions of 'Yuan' or other currencies. It's the biggest robbery, in the history of China…

And yet, the entire media realized: "The robbery that had occurred was not a coincidence."

Right this moment seen Aaron is mid-flight again, carrying this girl at the back. Though this pair unaware that many people on the ship and on dry land have watched him flying.

From shock, they're begun screaming in accord: "This is Sky Lord, who come to us from Heaven!"

Aaron and the girl withdrawn of that area; have traveled toward Changchun. Hours later those two have boarded a ferry, which taken them back to Chinese's Mainland; they were cruising to reach Guangzhou (or Canton).

Days later, Aaron seen is in midair, contrary of flying en route of the plane; he has turned sharply to the West. Later he was in the direction of the Chinese Mounts.

Flying quite a while, Aaron's strength failed him, so he thought: 'I feel weaker. My whole body is covered with sweat.'

Despite he's gasped for oxygen; but resumed talking: "We've to fly as far as possible from Tibet. Still, it's a strong wind blowing!"

Later that day, Aaron has remained in midair, is carrying Yuan Lu at his spinal.

Before long, Aaron was able to handle the situation under control; has kept flying farther away.

In no time what so ever; Aaron flew with this girl at his spinal, over the Pacific.

In few hours Aaron advanced to dry land, and has flown over the forestry, except he's been avoiding public sites. On the way, he reflects on it: "What if I haven't got enough strength to fly a long distance? Even to reach a Christmas-tree, which I spotted from a distant?"

There's sighted, the forest ended. Next up and beyond the horizon be with clear view, where has appeared long-drawn-out over the field.

In someplace seem its stuck smokestacks. The pair watched from above those peasants working in the fields; seeing they're heads ducked down.

Meanwhile, the locals frozen have amazed with open-mouthed or escaped from a shock or after; many others fell to the ground: "This is Sky Lord over, who come to safe us!"

Later Aaron into decisive thinking, in a life-threatening situation he's touched on: "If I tumble, we'll die in the water! I've strained my last strength for…"

On the spot, be loud, he ordered the girl: "Yuan Lu, hold on to me, as hard as you can!"

Out of space, something sprang, and has reflected in his mind: "I hope she doesn't fall off my back? One way or the other, I'll save her, the boy and myself, whatever the cost would-be! We'll definitely all meet!"

Carrying this girl behind, Aaron has flown through storms, rains and foggy - been heading for unknown destiny.

Chapter 14

MEANWHILE, in Monastery right this minute Fiend portrays for Brian of the latest: 'Aaron, together with this boy, Yuan Lu and a stranger, will be looking for food and drinks? True or not?'

Evildoer nodded, is responding: "Probably!"

Fiend is following next, when said: "And we can send Chinese police to search for those four! But we've to be involved with hundreds of locals to catch them? And we'll promise a reward to those farmers?"

Fiend finds himself 'in hot water'. Subsequently Brain gets up of his sit; and prevents Fiend from talking. He then overtakes discussion: "I confess, Xian Wei has deceived us! And yes, this was my fault! But, who would have thought he knew how pretending or simulate? I don't regret putting money into fixing his problem? Only with the assistance from those London Lawyers Bickering and Crofter." Fiend gestured him to silence.

Unexpectedly Brian walks up to the table; gets to a draw of a stylish desk, and opens it, seen is relaxed. Afterward he raises his hand, in which held a telegram: "Hum, I forgot to tell, I informed the Lawyers in London! Today I've received their reply, telegram where it's read: Bickering flies here on airplane. I think tomorrow, he'll reach China."

But neither Fiend, nor the others knew that Aaron and Yuan Lu flew to Northeast.

Meanwhile, somewhere in Northwest countryside, Aaron seems accomplished his purpose, was escaping with this girl.

Whilst saw Andrew beside Song Chuan were having embarked on the return flight of this aircraft that brought earlier to China Bickering.

The horizon stretched over meadow. Somewhere it has stuck smokestacks. This duo saw those peasants working in the fields, when their heads ducked down, and they remained with open-mouthed in astonishment, others fell to the ground, or run away.

They saw Aaron kept flying for some time; but accidentally he began gasping, as if being out of breath. Raindrops mixed with drops of sweat blow in his face.

He's felt that no longer has strength to fly with the girl behind: "I'm no longer able to fly with a load at my back? Yuan Lu, it's crucial for us to have a rest!"

Aaron finds himself in a danger, when began plunging down; against all odds intuitively he was looking for a shelter, in the Chinese Mountains.

When night advanced, has covered the sky that fell below and blackened the forest, near to which been seen a bright area, most likely laid of grass.

Those two went down on top by the stream with a grown tree and tangled rings. There seen young shoots of cane, amidst surrounding trees.

It was in a nook, where they can relax without fear of been seen by the strangers.

Aaron still was panting from exhaustion, after he's untied the ropes, and finally has freed Yuan Lu. What a relief it was, after letting her step on the ground.

On this occasion be down on the ground, in a flash Yuan Lu jumped from behind, fell down in front of Aaron; and trying to embrace his legs: "You're Sky Lord, who come from Heaven to safe me? Thank you, God!"

Aaron stood smiling forlornly; lifting up girl's chin, he began patting her hair. But him be frank: "I didn't expect that reaction from you? I'm not a God! You and I both poor people, and yet, we're fugitives!" Again he is stroking her head; and is ongoing: "Hush, hush, Yuan Lu! I'm like you a human, and very happy to survive, you too must be grateful! Now, lie down, and have a rest, I know you tired! And don't forget, tomorrow we're flying again. Do you approve, Yuan Lu?"

She subconsciously is overwhelmed, hearing his explanation. Despite Aaron's reason, this girl amazed: "Still it's good to have another God praising to?"

Although she's too tired considering now of anew strategy, been half-sleep. Aaron carefully folded a towel, and has laid it under Yuan Lu's head. Seen this girl instantly has fallen asleep, once her head slipped against the towel.

Later, when nightfall has reached peripheral; glow appears around the dark forestry, which lightened up white clouds, passing in front of the moon.

Aaron couldn't sleep, be seated on turf, in the middle of nowhere: "Despite my fatigue, I cannot sleep? I'm too excited!" He stops talking.

Next Aaron logically: "It's sensation of nocturnal influence, perhaps this comes from nearby garden? By a mixture of weird sweet-spicy aroma from the flowers?"

He has penetrated to the very heart of restless; as walking in fear at the thoughts of possible proximity to people it's risky; despite they're at the Himalayas Mountain.

A sudden fresh gust of wind starts pulling from the ground, and strip of a white mist, covered like a blanket, across Chinese mainland surroundings.

Chapter 15

AT this very moment, saw Aaron beside Yuan Lu have landed; and climbed into thick grounds, without they're thinking of treacherous snakes, and such like of these insects being around.

Days later Aaron alongside Yuan Lu's have reunited with Song Chuan and Andrew, in neighboring village by the hills that was detached from Chinese province, where they would-be hardly hunted.

Many days passed, since those four have arrived in Chinese Changchun. Then one day, after consuming breakfast, this quartet made their way near main road.

They come to view a picturesque site, where onward, in a grove amid trees have been seen one of the tropical, which rare to be found, but covered with turf huts.

Time-in-between local Chinese hanged decorations with red lights on walls, and around their places. It's popular on this period got around the Chinese New Year, which has been celebrated across China, and beyond.

Time flew by for this quartet; it's all happened on Sunday, at Market day; where saw under the tree sits a Monk, like skeleton of a large looking Chinese man.

He's hair shaved; and he is playing a wooden flute. This man is puffing out his cheeks, but it seems he would burst air out.

Song Chuan on recess, is half-whispering, but looked bold: 'Brother, Bo, can you see a crowd afar? They surrounded the snake charmer plying a pipe?'

Walking into a crowd, in front of them appears a skinny boy who is showing tricks to audience with three cups and a ball. Seen those peasants have thrown small coins in his plate, only few penises. RMB currencies - 'Yuan' were carried out, only in pockets of the richest.

Nearby appears those women-merchants are wearing colorful clothes, which seen on stall where they've sold colorful fabrics, and much more.

On the spot those four noticed a blind beggar with a wooden bowl in his hands, and he is screaming: "Good people, take pity on me? God helps you, then give me a handful of your money, please?"

As there are having performed squirm accounts, the singing beggars, executed on flutes, thundering drums, bleating goats, roared horses, screaming toddlers.

There saw women vendors wore ethnic group old-fashioned, mainly red, while selling stuff.

Passing by, this quartet sights adjacent a vendor kept screaming: "Tea! Chai! How about green tea, do you want it?"

It's inflamed the small Song Chuan's eyes; and he pulled hand out. Having a chance Yuan Lu turns toward Aaron; is asking: "Brother Bo, let's go in the crowd where those broods play with toys? I envy them! Look at this girl, she is forgotten everything, and blows a shrill whistling. Look, her parents bought her red whistle, and a doll?"

Aaron too stares at stuff that happens spellbound him: "I'm fascinated by that spectacle? After a sedating silence, and boring life in Monastery, this blinding, cheerful light, with colors fascinates me! Most exciting of all those locals could freely move? And all this is intoxicating!"

An hour later, in meadow, by gateway to the village, those four appear are walking across piercing, to an established Chinese Market.

There a vendor tried to attract customers, when is yelling: "Come here, good people! I have fruits for you to bargain!"

Following another vendor is yelling to attract customers: "Fresh cheese! Rose petal water! Come here, and buy!"

Aside, the next vendor's seen in the fish stalls, displays his products: "Fish! Fresh carps, I've caught them today, come and buy!"

Apart, close to the exit, a teen vendor, and another seller are shouting: "Garlands of flowers, buy from here! I've desirable dried plants!"

Aloud have touted passers-by, poor dressed broods; huddled near the sellers of toys and whistles made of palm leaves, colored sticks, wooden rattles, dolls, glass.

Sudden from nowhere heard noises, with a sharp sound of car horns, coming from the road.

Breaking through a crowd toward the market, slowly drove up a vehicle, splashed with mud. In it sat two men, wearing dark-color European-made suits.

A car has braked. Out of the car appear two policemen with cameras crashed into a crowd, which respectfully parted before them, leaving wide passage. They began walking rapidly - directly toward Aaron.

Caution returned to him, and in a dangerous situation he's squeezed both Song Chuan's and Yuan Lu hands. Aaron finds himself in jeopardy; and began thinking: "Is it a chase?"

Recalling what horrors he's experienced in the Monastery... Aaron begun walking away fast, is led those broods away to the grove; although it's not easy to break through a solid crowd. It seems the Police be closing in.

Aaron does a sudden somersault; and grabs this boy, like a doll; he then goes in midair. Those Chinese witnessed all that have occurred.

On the spot, Aaron turns head to the side, where this air-motorbike be placed in an exclusive space covered with glass.

Song Chuan understood his plan, equally nods his head. He's in a life-threatening moment shaken his head: 'No, Brother, don't fly!' Song Chuan delays, has obstructed Aaron's flight with his hands; but he lifts up without thinking. In extreme danger, Aaron attempts flying.

Once this boy, saw that a policeman pointed a gun at Aaron; instinctively he's anxiously shouting: "Oh, no! God, help us! Xian Wei!"

Aaron, meanwhile is aerial, still held Song Chuan in his hands, but is on the brink of dropping the boy down.

By taken his full strength, he's seized Song Chuan close to his chest. Aaron finds himself in extreme danger: abruptly began tumbling. Luckily he and the boy don't fall to the ground.

He is clattering down fast, and come within reach of a air-motorbike, and sneaked forward in an attempt to fly away, Aaron's hung over in midair, like an acrobat.

Aaron and this boy have jumped inside air-motorbike. Now brought to the attention the quartet is in air-motorbike, but seen Aaron reclined aside on this Exhibition for demonstration.

Andrew, meantime, without delay turns to start the flying motorbike, and presses gas to gain speed. He then nods his head, said: "Attention! We can go for the flying variation, how's this sounds, kids?"

Seeing a life-threatening situation, the policeman removes a gun, and fires in the air. Made it gunshots, policeman missed by ten inches, when has targeted straight into the flying air-motorbike.

Meantime, without having experience of handling the air-motorbike, Andrew has twitched on its engine, with Aaron's help. It's a life-threatening situation; he is pressing on gas to start machinery air navigating.

In split-second once the air-motorbike takeoff, and flew fast, like someone has chased it. It's been dangerous for those four; but Andrew kept pressing on gas. Succeeding in his effort machine begun orbiting, elevating higher and higher; until seen it's flying away.

It's been critical moment, looked gap between the group of four that is flying in air-motorbike, and the local police, which couldn't do much about.

In mid course, Aaron decides under Andrew's supervision not cutting air supply to conduct the flight that is held almost horizontally control of air-motorbike.

The quartet was in-midair a while; when Song Chuan begun suddenly screaming on top of his lungs: "Oh, no! Spirit, fly away!"

This boy saw danger, because of an approaching plane, since they've stolen apparatus from a display. In extreme circumstance, saw he and Yuan Lu have clutched hands, up on their chests, and both kids are frightened.

Aaron attempts inside conduct machinery flying faster. Yuan Lu meantime is licked her lips, and looked desperate: "I'm thirsty! I want to drink?"

Aaron, turns see to her, but shakes his head: "No, Yuan Lu! You can't have a drink now! Wait until we out of foes view! When we'll land, then find you water, is it a deal?"

Be a modest girl, Yuan Lu, nodded, and puts a grin for him: "Okay, wise man!"

To their hardship Song Chuan begun wheezing; still gave a smile; then he has admitted: "I'm scared, but you all can depend on me!"

For the time being seen air-motorbike picked up height, is flown to remote area.

At some stage of quartet's flight on air-motorbike that was fast ascending, while Andrew is sped, conducting the airlift.

Andrew was piloting; seems being on course for woodland. Those four were flying in machinery on altitude, a whole day in row, till night debarked. Those four are admiring, while having witnessed picturesque red-blood twilight.

Mutually agreeing, Andrew and Aaron are having decided for air-motorbike landing in this part of China, which located nigh low-valley in Himalayas Mounts. Andrew was kept piloting the flight, often swapping places with Aaron.

Before long those four traveled aboard air-motorbike: all of a sudden it's begun tumbling toward the ground, neither Aaron nor Andrew were able piloting this aeronautical.

They tried to delay; but the machinery plunged in-midair; traveled towards a huge tree-trunk; lucky it didn't crash.

Half-hour later after they've landed, Andrew looked tense; yet is elated: "The four of us can have a rest there. We'll sleep on the ground. Aaron, tell the kids, what I said?"

"Song Chuan, I know you're tired, it's getting cold, and we need shrubs. Please, go and collect some." Bid Aaron.

This boy nods his head; and rapidly gets up of the ground: "Yes, brother Bo! I'm going at once!"

Once Song Chuan walked off; Aaron spins to look at the girl he's carried; then instructs her:

"Yuan Lu, make yourself comfortable, down on lawn. And get ready to sleep!"

This girl tags on herself with a blanket they've picked up in machinery; puts a smile, and reacted: "Yes, brother Bo, I'm tired! And I'm going to sleep!"

Chapter 16

MANY days have passed, since Aaron and his friends fled Monastery. On this particular morning, in Monastery, Fiend is reading comments in local newspaper, of the event that had taken place at Changchun's exposition. Surprisingly, he's noticed a photo included, and his eyes caught a newspaper article...

"So Aaron, Song Chuan, Yuan Lu and the stranger were there? But, to what destination they flew, afterwards?" - Guessed Fiend.

Fiend thought with fear of a scandal that will resolves to be erupted with Evildoer.

Shortly Brian's reaction wasn't long awaited to explode: "The same people, who have caught the birds, where feeders it's silk." He's silent; and began breathing deeply; he then is saying: "Fiend, don't fool yourself thinking I'll forget about it? We'll return to this conversation later."

Few days later, Fiend sent to Chinese newspaper an article, where he has reported of phenomenal event witnessed by many people. The article was in the local newspaper's editor, which published a note: 'Our special correspondent visited the scene, and has interviewed witnesses. According to him we're dealing with a clever invention or a new wingless aircraft? Further investigation of a mysterious Flying man, is conducted, if it's false a report of the flying man stolen a boy and a girl, in daylight, when he was accompanying by some, these rumors have to be established?'

No one knew that Fiend was the most interested party in it, and a liar.

This story was reprinted in other newspapers with diverse interpretations, and has provoked a lot of controversies.

Finally, Chinese magazines with conservative view used this mind-blowing story, by cliché: 'A God, and the society raised Religious fanaticism, to promote Dalai Lama...'

The articles in other magazines have inscribed: 'Will a reasonable person of the twentieth Century, believe any young men in daylight, could steal a girl, in front of the crowd, like a hawk the chicken? Still flying, after he was grabbing a boy too? Witnesses convinced it was abductions of the children, we must know how, many children were abducted by this person?'

Other Chinese newspaper "The Society" is credulous that it's believed: "The great mysteries of Levitation brought miracles for centuries! A young man, is possibly a new incarnation of the immortal?"

Next weekly wrote: "A Man appeared on Earth to strengthen a falling religion? If you've doubts, a well-known professor wrote 'As scientists could express their opinion, only the facts that count'! I can only say that, I never witnessed levitation, if in modern science of research specifying a hypothetical explanation of such miracles?"

There hasn't been long coming a disagreement between the conflicting sides. Hours later, Evildoer went to Fiend having a hot temper; so furious he's never seen Brian who worked as the Head of Monastery's Theosophists.

It's heard he is shouting at Fiend: "Dens, I'll throw you out not only from this Monastery, but far from China too! You stupid, and a bloody scatterbrain!"

Fiend in an attempt to maintain peace: "Sir, you so angry that it could light up a candle out off you..."

On a critical point, Evildoer interrupts Fiend: 'Mostly you alone responsible for all that occurred! And you're to be blamed for its consequences! Where were your praised sessions of hypnosis, which hold tight Aaron in the iron chain?' Though he's shushed for a jiffy. Evildoer then prolonged: "What we're going to tell Crofter and Bickering?"

Brian picks up a newspaper, and points inside: "Now, how to cope with the noise that were raised by many newspapers?"

To miss this trump card out of his hands, Fiend tired to cry. Dens find himself in hot water. At last calms down slightly; he's settling it, in a steady voice: "Brian, we know whereabouts Aaron and those kids were, cause he can't fly far with a weight behind his back? Can't you see it's impossible?

'Aaron obviously wouldn't carry easily a boy and a girl? Don't forget, he cannot fly fast enough, as well long distances? And Aaron wouldn't leave those kids either! Trust me, we will catch them, one way or the other!"

Brian swiftly has interrupted Fiend: "For this alone you must do all the catches and flying, like Aaron. I'm telling you, it's impossible! Get him, Dens, it's like, 'to catch the bird, flown away from the cage'!"

He became silent for a jiffy. Then on a critical moment, Evildoer picks up a glass of water, and drank strait-up.

Fiend takes a chance, to prove his motives: "And when Aaron with the broods are to be caught, the whole story will be treated as a joke! And the newspapers would be left with nothing, more than rumors?"

Brian seems is skeptical, and not convinced: 'If I only can share your optimism? What if Aaron is forced to tell the whole bloody story? No flying man lost to this Monastery? Aaron and those broods must be caught! But if the public discovers the real story, our Institution may be closed for good, and we could...'

In a flash, Fiend intruded: "And we could be put to the Dock? What if he'll report us to the authorities?" He then looks up at Brian.

Evildoer instead gave a sneer; and declared: "Do you think I'll be silent about what's happened in here? Cause I've decided to appear in Court, Mr. Fiend!"

Dens on a whim is earnest: "Are you really sure, Evildoer? You wouldn't dare?"

Evildoer appears calm cool and collective, when in his turn talks by sharp tone: "Try me? I've nothing to lose!

'As you said, in England they're aware of the situation here. You'll get to learn, what the greatest Confucius taught, he was known to the world of being wise, when said 'Careful, it's danger'!" In a critical moment, Evildoer has made a point; but remains of fret: "Dens, I hope you didn't forget your past, when you were free from the prison? Back at those years ago you were keen for asylum, and had found refuge in this Monastery? During your so-called career as a leading Teacher 'Guru', you've driven by affairs in here. And yet, you turned into a perpetrator without doubt. Strangely you became a preacher of Universal Love, and mercy? 'Ha-ha-ha! I've researched all about you. And I'm not talking about your multiple uses of activities in Monastery? Let's have a guess: how many broods were abducted on your orders from their parents? Most important: how you had driven those children to suicide, and ruined their lives? I have all these recorded!"

They looked at each other, like two cocks in the face of a new battle. Prudence has prevailed: Evildoer slapped Fiend over his left shoulder.

Fiend gave a smirk; and is acted in respond, in a sarcastic tone: "We're both guilty! But we must not quarrel. Since we need to get out of the situation without dirt, Master of 'Buddha'? I'm sure it wouldn't last long. And when Aaron is in our hands, apparently it would be best to end this... We have to get rid of him!"

Although Evildoer interrupts him, and his tongue in cheek: "If or when he falls in our hands, Dens?"

A sudden Brian gets-up of his sit has stretched his body, taken a rest; then forms a smile: "Now, lets think of a plan for upcoming result, and of our joint actions, Fiend?"

Meanwhile, the next morning Andrew appears when has helped first Song Chuan prepare. Once he's placed this boy inside air-motorbike; next is calling on Yuan Lu, who's swiftly jumped into the machinery.

In quirk of fate, they've four got a wish: touching top of the sky... Once the air-motorbike flew, and already is in the direction of the Himalayan Mountains.

Erratically this flying machinery starts plummeting...

At some stage of air travel, Aaron, alongside three nomads was within reach of highland; where on the spot, they've decided landing in that quiet part of China.

After those four were out of a flying apparatus; as stepping out it seems their feet be shaky, they disembark on solid ground. There they end-up in unfamiliar territory for chitchat.

In next to no time those four were en route, walking some miles to unknown... It's been time on the brink of evening, in this part of China, where now seen a gloomy night.

Seems climate has changed: its erratically begun gushing rain, dropping faster and faster. Following of a thunder that resonances be heard across this province.

Without delay Andrew ties Yuan Lu, as she set on Aaron's spinal. Following Song Chuan is fixed.

Guessing he's life under threat carrying two kids behind, Aaron is decided: "No, I cannot carry both of the children. I'd rather take for the ride Yuan Lu. And you, Andrew, take Song Chuan with you again!"

Aaron determines in a difficult situation fly, and carrying Yuan Lu at his spinal. While Andrew waits for his return, to lift up this boy next.

Before they're flying-off Aaron's fasten her tight at his back with ropes, since the girl isn't heavy, it's a good thing.

Meantime, Aaron goes again in midair with Yuan Lu's tied at his back; but is listening carefully to upcoming noises.

Later the young four eventually reunified; and are walking another few miles...

At long last a group of four have approached countryside, without knowing where they are.

Spotting from a distant, a glimpse of light to be on, in woodshed, this gave an indication that someone is inside, maybe user-friendly?

This shed belonged to a family of three, in which Wu Tang was the oldest man of the house, being in his late sixties. Yet, the breadwinner in this family be a young woman, his daughter. She's barely nineteen years of age, named Wu Lan, very slim, been decently dressed, has medium-short height; and with long black hair, which braided the braid.

In Chinese tradition of respect, Master of the house Wu Tang has invited this hungry quartet, to have dinner with his wife, and daughter Wu Lan. Those four appear are seated at the table near Wu Tang, his wife, with their daughter on the other side, and all consuming plain rise with fried beef.

Hearing discussion between three adults of these groups', as they've spoken English during dinnertime.

The next day saw Aaron's spoken confidentially to Andrew: "I want to shed light on the phishing scams, which those Lawyers slash Guardians have made me undergo; it was true hell, in Monastery,"- he's expression has suddenly changed to grim. To that Andrew comes back with rationality: "Aaron, don't worry punishing them, Christina and I've made certain steps that Lawyers will get, what they deserve jail! Now, we've to focus on your safety, till a chance arises for you're going to England?"

The day after, it's revised to a view of glorious morning with sunlit. Meantime, in Wu Tang's shed seen the owners' have welcomed this quartet from previous nights, to sleep over.

Aaron alongside Andrew and those kids have got up and about at dawn, seen they slipped on outfits, ensuing are wearing coats on, still there's frosty outside.

But for Yuan Lu who's wearing a skirt is too large, she's trapped, which prevent her been mobile. Seen atop she's worn a warm long jumper, a gift from Wu Lan.

Soon, those four shifted outside, where in close proximity to shed set a place for washing up; but underfoot they've sensed turf ground; while the soil felt cool, but soggy.

Those four immediately joined a queue, waiting for their turn to come for washing up. This group of four pithily is having washed they're faces, brushed teethes, and combed their hair.

At lunchtime, Wu Tang has invited those four to eat lunch with his family and him. At get-together, this owner warned them: "Don't go to the neighboring mansion of the local Star, film director Shui Qing."

Many days following their trip were over, after this group of four landed there. Those four were captivated by amazing view that took their breath away: having looked around, both been rapt by near the canal's deep end. However, this Estate belonged to film director Shui Qing.

Meanwhile, Andrew is chewing the fat with Aaron, standing near massive waterway that separated this village from the forest. Andrew gave honest account; yet somewhat worried him: "You know we've stuck in deep shit, Aaron! We can't travel any longer, because they're hunting you! What we're going to do?"

With similar idea as Andrew Aaron wishfully thinking to have new plan. Andrew disrupts his thoughts: "Why the hell, did you go to this garden?"

Aaron's responded spontaneously: "Sorry, I was curious."

Resulting Andrew explains to him the outcome: "As people say 'curiously killed a cat'! If you refuse to accept Shui Qing's contest, the police could catch us? And they'll take you back to Monastery! And God knows what could happen to those kids and me? You don't have a choice, as to accept it, Aaron!"

Aaron talks sensitively: "A wise man said 'No-one can escape their destiny!' Do you think we can fly far away?" He became silent; though is gasping for air.

Andrew's reaction logical: "Who knows? Damn it, I forgot, it's too heavy for you to carry both kids behind? And we don't have money for traveling?"

Chapter 17

ANOTHER day of freedom and survival passes for the four; this time it's become terrifying that strikes at midday.

From nowhere came into view a dragon flew above the film director, Shui Qing's Estate, this monster isn't huge, but it's being seeking for the prey.

Shui Qing meantime, curtsies, as a form of respect; but is ironic: "This dragon has long claws, and its eyes like be made of glass. So far, no one came out alive, battling the monster!" He clams up; gave a smirk; and prolonged: "Did know my dragon called Lord of the Sky?"

Aaron interrupts him: "And I was called by locals, Angel! I'll cope with it!"

Time-in-between, the dragon saw a dump, where a man stood down unprotected without a shield. It's spine-chilling; seen this monster has burnt him to a crisp.

Aaron has remained at the film director's land; when begun talking, but is cynical: "Mister Shui Qing, this dragon's indicated on one's last meal, before the execution of its prey?"

A Chinese man's lowered neck back, he's laughter resonated: "Why would you think that, Xian Wei? We're not barbarians, here!"

In life-threatening situation, Aaron turns to look around; seems he is grumpy, when is murmuring: "No matter how, but your enemies know where we're? Yet, we under surveillance."

Before long, Aaron on the scene is in midair, while flown back. Be in extreme danger he grabs a polished shield that shines like a mirror, set aside. This time he pictures of the danger: "I must think of the best tactic to attack this dragon?"

Despite Aaron was shielded; but soon he's being wounded by dragon's claw; all the same he doesn't feel the pain.

It's nigh lethal, Aaron's got exhausted; in such condition he talks to himself: "I wish I'm a giant to defeat this bloody monster-dragon?"

Prevailing, on the ground, are perceived wobbly noises of a choir: "Ohm-ohm!"

Sudden action by a dragon called 'Lord of the Sky', spewed fire from its jaw in the air, with thunderous echoes that's sound be heard across.

Aaron felt heat from dragon's surge of fire; it has nearly caught him. Yet, he's fought back, whilst flying fast.

On the way Aaron corners to grab a polished shield this has shined like a mirror; in his turn is determined to attack the dragon from behind, in-midair; and he's crept forward.

Promptly Aaron has become alarmed from shock: "I wish this dragon could see its own reflection in a shining shield that I'm holding?"

Without losing a second, clash between Aaron and the dragon is begun, in midair.

Everyone present witnessed that battle, as they've on the spot high-pitched, they were scared-stiff of this enormous monster-creature's power.

"Every second counts,"- thought Aaron; and goes in-midair, where he looks like an arrow. Yet he's tumbled rapidly, as if is landing.

Impulsively, Aaron jumped up on dragon's neck, fastens it around with a wire. Though this dragon resists, when it's swiftly attempted to throw Aaron, who's tumbled, as if is falling down; but he's resilient.

Turning back and forth, Aaron's surprisingly noticed Wu Lan amongst that crowd. Without losing time, he raises in-midair; has straightened himself like an arrow; and tumbles down, as if is landing.

Before he grabs Wu Lan she curtsies modestly, and yells: "Yes, Sky Lord, do retaliate!"

Aaron holds the girl by a dress; next flies away with her. Everyone is in disbelief.

Shortly, Aaron has landed in Shui Qing's garden. Next he moved to a tent; where is talking to Wu Lan: "There's no the time to talk. I'll come to see you, later!"

She curtsies modestly, as sign of respect: "Yes, Sky Lord, I'll wait for you!"

Time has appeared close to midnight. There came into view Wu Lan, who has fast approached outskirts of the village. She is anxiously observing the sky, waiting for Aaron's return.

Soon Wu Lan has noticed him flying, and is become excited. Aaron too saw her, and directly is begun landing nearby her standing.

Despite Aaron is keen to speak with her, but doesn't forget of danger that he has found himself in; and of serious outcomes, which they are facing be in someone estate.

On the spot he is uttering to her: "Oh, Wu Lan! What were you doing in Shui Qing's mansion?"

In next to no time they were seated down; and Aaron breaks silence: 'I have it all under control, Wu Lan.'

They hooked on, evolving intimate for them alone, as this pair of loving birds began passionately kissing.

Aaron seems be concerned, for its crucial that she accepted his strategy.

'Why you need to leave, darling? Its part of your tactic for disperse that will happen soon?' Attentively has asked Wu Lan.

"Maybe. Do you agree with my tactic? Wu Lan, will you wait for me?" Asked Aaron. She converts to silence, and thought awhile. With admiration for Aaron, she's enlightened him with her promise: "Yes!"

He's suggested: 'I'm taken you back, Wu Lan. Go to your friends, and stay with them overnight.'

It's developed cockcrow; spur-of-the-moment Aaron's like a ghost struggled to leave Qing's Estate; he's lucky a camera wasn't installed there.

Soon after, Aaron has detached earlier; still only a minute was left for him, before he flies away without being caught on the spot in this pavilion.

In the middle of the road, he's met Andrew. From nowhere, emerged a 'BMW'; vehicle suddenly breaks near where those two stood.

As the car-door opens-up, from inner steps out Shui Qing; and approaches Aaron, then without preamble: "Have you called for a vehicle by a chance? If the police chase after you, no doubt they'll catch you!"

Aaron senses as if has got trapped; he stared from shock; and became pale.

Shui Qing speaks in a biting wit: 'Listen, whatever your name is? Why is not give the police a call, where to find the Flying man? You don't mind, Xian Wei, if I ring them about you? Why you've turned pale now, my young friend?'

Aaron finds himself in a dangerous situation; and said in a low-slung; but he is apprehensive: "I'm the Flying man, you right! So, what are you going to do about it, mister Shui Qing?"

Shui Qing shakes with his neck, is reacted: "You've defeated my dragon, so you must work for me!"

Aaron interrupts him, resulting gave a sneer; he's tongue-in-cheek: "The Buddha stated 'Hope for the best. Prepare for the worst. And expect nothing!' I'm Sky Lord, and make decisions without be forced. I need to consider."

Once Shui Qing left, Aaron's been joined by Andrew, whilst they have remained on open-air for a chat. Aaron has turned to look around, for safety reason.

Seems Andrew's edgy, thus is low-voicing: "From the time, when four of us have fallen under surveillance… But we all have to keep a low profile, and been quiet."

A minute ago saw Chang, who is Qing's watchdog and worked as an informer to the police: come within reach of the two; and budges into their chat. A watchdog with unorthodox behavior seems to be prying, when is asked the two: "Whom are you talking about?"

Aaron looks at Andrew nervously. But Greenwood gave a smirk; and alleged, be sarcastic: "Gee, let me think? I was talking about this same bloody thing Shui Qing!"

Once Chang left; Aaron prolongs: 'Shui Qing will not make money out of my ability, or see me killed!' His eyewinks, as if was confidant; seen Aaron's shoulders shuddered.

Though he has sensed danger; on the spot decided to fly as far as possible. Seen Andrew is following Aaron; and those two are walking away.

In an extreme, Aaron decided: "While those kids are safe and protected by Wu Lan and her father? Now I've to think about my own safety, and fly as far away from here, as possible."

From the moment when Aaron's taken off, has soared far and wide; and flown as fast as he could.

On the way he would listen warily; is watching around. Seen he is flying toward a tall building, the high-rise.

At some stage of Aaron's flight, it's a good thing that he was not seen by anyone, except for some skyscrapers, where security-cameras have been installed.

Chapter 18

AT this moment, the weather in China follows the calendar, as a transitional period in step: summer's gone, timely for autumn.

At present outside it's developed hours of darkness, where seen the sky been full of shooting stars.

Despite in this period saw early autumn, it felt warm, in that forsaken part of the world was thrived, thanks to mixture of a tropical climate there.

Soon the night has vanished; it's opened a view of a lovely sunrise in this part of Chinese mainland that was close to low-gorge of the Himalayan Mounts.

Meanwhile, somewhere in the Himalayan Mount existed a local Buddhist Temple. Secluded, and far be unbolted a sight of the Prophecy, not related to Church; there was set a pavilion. Around that area Aaron has made stopover.

Days later, it's seen a dawn in Himalayan Mountains, where at open-air developed a fog that has covered like a blanket through wide-ranging zone.

On a whim Aaron turns to observe the location, like is in search for something that will give him a tip-off.

A rumor has it that, in Himalayan Mountain exists orchid-epiphytic flower?

A sudden wind-gush scared Aaron; has made him tumbledown. It's obscured and could have fragmented, in which finally been composed. Afterwards Aaron starts elevating again.

Almost a month had passed, from the time when Aaron landed in that territory of the Himalayan Mountains. In this part of China, current time is on the verge of midnight, and it has sensed a frosty weather.

From time to time Aaron thought: "What I should do next?" Utmost he's thriving: "I've held residence in this Temple, where the Buddhists can come to worship their God, Buddha?" He shushes fast; sucks in air. He looks as if is superior over all this. Although he contradicts himself, is talking in jingle: "But I can fly! As I'm the Sky Lord!" He clams up; inhales; and talks more to himself: "In Monastery, I learned only pretending, and to hide my real feelings! How I've to act now?"

This fear drove Aaron in the woods, deprived the company of people, where among them were good, for him it's doomed to isolation there.

One day, a Monk appeared before Aaron, and has touched his shoulder, he said: "What's troubling you, young man?"

Despite concern, Aaron decided to open-up: "I was fleeing Tibet, and coming to Himalayan mounts, but here I live in fear to be back in enemies hands?"

This Monk looks at him, and said: "I don't know your problems? But Buddha was suffering too. And he's declared - All birds find shelter during a rain. But Eagle avoids rain by flying above the clouds. Problems are common, but Attitude makes the difference.' Now, you a Man, do you know what your next move is?"

Aaron seems is unsure: "I didn't consider taken some sort of action be free-for-all, and to defend my right to exist."

The Monk smiles, has explained: "Here's Buddha's resolution 'Because you are alive, everything is possible!' Now you've realized?"

"Lest if I want it, not the normal way of life than others do?" There he heard some black bears cry, before animals suppose to go for a long winter sleep.

Sudden something woke his human pride; by exasperation: "No, I couldn't stay in this rain-forest any longer! I'll fly to be with human and get my rights to live among them! Why shouldn't I use my extraordinary gift? Be the Flying man, I can do a lot for them! What exactly? I've no idea, or even knew a little of their lives? However time will tell itself what I should do? 'Time don't wait for nor men or women,' as the Chinese say." Reflected Aaron, and has begun, at once put his thoughts together.

When out of the blue, he's decided changing his name to Cecil, with a Chinese name Xiang Bo. With such look, Aaron could not be mistaken for a Chinese man, quite the reverse, it's shown his appearance have been a European.

Without delay, Aaron began preparations for long journey. Seeming several lightened without bathing, he was remained fair skinned.

He examined his shirt and bed sheet, and has washed these, whilst the sun-heated the rocks, he's tried to smooth them, and get it dry. His skin look tanned.

Aaron was having handful of apples in his bosom he ripped earlier, with rucksack. And he takes off one morning for a lengthy flight, where to destiny will take him.

Chapter 19

ONE morning, somewhere in China's province become known a priest, who's baptized Nicolas Roberts, is having coffee at the courtyard, of the Church. He seems in a middle-aged crisis man, tall, has mane brushed with grey; and wears over his pajamas. He's called by a Chinese name Wang Chou.

For a while Nicolas was looking at hanged cross-of an Amulet with a sign, thinking: "That's all, who they were? On the chest dangled the Cross-and-amulet. What's next?"

"Wang Chou, you seem to be far away?" A loud woman's voice echoed, brought this cleric back to wits; it has come from the Church.

Now he became attentive: 'What if it was the local Chinese, listening to God's message and wished to be baptized?'

"Nicolas, someone is waiting for you…"- she couldn't finish sentence.

Forgetting finishing breakfast, this priest swiftly puts on a long black robe over his pajamas; and is hurried towards ingress.

Contrary, in front of Nicolas stood a slender light-skinned lad, is good-looking, and he has long hair hermit, but he smelled awfully. This young man was wearing only a shirt and a strange grayish cloak.

"Did you want to see me?" In contrast, has raised his voice the priest.

To the priest's surprise, Uriel spoke in a perfect London intonation: "Yes, sir!" Humbly and quietly responded this lad; see his eyes downcast.

"I meant priest, I'd like talk to you. My apology, if I've disturbed you?"

Later Nicolas invited this newcomer, (who is Aaron), to his Church office; and has learned that he come here for a serious talk.

A visitor: "I'm called Xiang Bo. But I'm Chinese orphan." Although his appearance told quite the opposite: he has looked-like a European; when said: 'I want to give myself to God's services! I'm educated, for instance Brahmanism studied Buddhism. I've learned Koran too, and Jewish studies, as a core. By all means, religion doesn't satisfy me...'- About Christianity Aaron knew well-enough; and said: "I'd like to look deeper into beliefs. What I don't like in the Religion is their countries oppressed others..."- Has added to his story Xiang Bo: "The fact is that their Gods doesn't reveal themselves, as it seems not come to the aid of individuals?" The preacher's frowned: "Tell me, what is your real, English name?"

Aaron without thinking responded: "Cecil! But I wouldn't tell my surname!"

But to itself Nickolas thought: "The man's got excellent education for a native, this hard to believe it? And his practical mind is superb."

Resulting Nicolas began talking: "Young man, it seems you require kind of shrewd signs, wonders, which is solid. Can you demonstrate existence of God that is the manifest? Have you been baptized, tell the truth?"

"No! To the extent that I recall, I've not!" He pretends to be called Xiang Bo.

The priest jumps in the discussion; is ongoing: "But can you show me apart from basic things: miracles, whatever the cost? For that you'll get a Silver Cross pendant gift from me that you must wear it! A report should develop in the new converts..."

The priest didn't finish talking, to his astonishment, Aaron called Cecil, starts elevating; is seen already ascent up to the top.

This came as a shock to Roberts, when Aaron ascended to the ceiling, and be hanged with his feet down, like God.

"Can we talk privately of your miracle, my friend?" Seems be wonderful, assumed the priest: "Such a phenomenon, we've never seen. Where do you live?"

"I'm a wanderer, reverend! Seeking true God!" Has reacted the stranger, who happens is Aaron, when suddenly begun elevating.

Roberts initial reaction, of an ideal specimen, silently: "What if the locals can see that miracle?"

A minute ago has emerged a nun called Magdalena, who stood aside. A priest began talking, when solemnly tackled Aaron: "We've a vacant chamber, and you can stay in our Church, Uriel!" After he turns attention to this nun: "We find a corner and a handful of rice for any man, who seek God! Yes, sister Magdalena?" He almost shouted at her.

Her real name was Margot; who appeared in the age of her thirties. She is wearing a brown long outfit kind of Monk robe that made of cotton or linen that covered her ankles. She has a medium-short hair; seen her head be covered with a bright shawl tied behind; a white lace went up and over her waist. She seems is frowned at her brotherly love, kneeling down; when Margot raises her head to look at Roberts; she swiftly walks-off.

Once an ash-blond-haired skinny woman returns, Margo has already changed from religious robe into a dress.

The priest declares with urgency: "This is Uriel. I hope he would-be your future Godson? He'll live in our Church. Take him to garret, please, sister Magdalena!"

Magdalena is nosily looking at Xiang Bo; and nodded: "Come on with me, lad!" Has called Magdalena on Aaron, in a way she's inclined her head towards the heavy door.

The priest meantime, removed his glasses, has sighed, and leaned back in his chair. Seen his eyebrows have risen; looking on the wall over the hearth, where has hung a picture of an England Lord, who was the Governor of Hong Kong, amid other portraits. Roberts was a priest, to be more specific: he's sermonized at the local Church. Conducting prayers for the native Chinese. As a priest he has inspired those on a Christian way, and predominantly every part of it, went successful.

Long ago, in the original reports Roberts had made clear the reason for his missionary activities success includes prudence and exertion.

Despite his effort preaching to those Chinese, the priest be criticized, he seems didn't meet expectations of Minster.

"Will be the reputation of this priest patronized, after he was reading the last justification?"

Three weeks in a row Roberts had pored over the report, and tried to present effects in a positive light, it's been in vain. The reason it's gone contradictory that, he was attracted to God's flock of sheep - 'Gentiles', on the poorest.

"Given that for those locals transition from Buddhism to Christianity was kind of promising. Several of them have improved their powerless positions!"

He believed was playing significant role, presenting locals with silver crosses that were cheap gifts, which they've got from him through Baptism.

"This could convert those local Chinese to Christianity?"

Except Roberts was wrong. Accordingly, many of the recluses have preferred cleansing baptism. Nonetheless, everything had changed for him. For that reason, Roberts stopped sermons in this Church.

As the priest tried to succeed in attracting new followers to the Church, he has failed, as it's become increasingly challenging mission. Due to reflections this was upsetting the priest, he's lost appetite, and been discreet of arisen situation.

During daytime, he worked up sweat on ingenious report. By nighttime, Roberts would invent tools that could improve to fight the 'evils spirits'.

This priest was an eloquent sermon, by which has made his missionary trips to the most remote Chinese villages and nearby Parishes, nothing improved so far.

Before China, he was a missionary in Central America, whereby these pagans and the fanatics could smell miracles, proving superiority of the Christianity. But Roberts has wondered, where to obtain a miracle?

With Aaron's arrival Roberts's found a sign to restore all that was problematic.

The next morning, a nun's voice awoke Nicolas: "Minister, go and have breakfast with Xiang Bo!"

Aaron hears her voice through the door. Aaron knew Margot was priest's close relative, a sister, when he introduced her earlier, and called her nun.

Unexpectedly approached a local girl is held a tray in her hands, where stood a steaming teapot, cups, and a plate with scrambled eggs on a toast. She's the Goddaughter of 'Sister Magdalena' (called a nun in the house of God to serve the priest) and the parishes.

Later, when they've left office in Church, Margot returned soon; and been frank: "Look, brother, I think you in your Missionary went too far, and zeal to forget simple? Don't put this beggar above the people from our Church? After all, this dirty nomad hotbeds can have infections, which brought in here?"- She said impatiently: "It's not enough that I was sick with tuberculosis? I was equally disease-ridden by cholera, and still lacking a full recovery! Even you with others can catch epidemic viruses from these birds?"

"Not a single hair falls from this man's head, without the will of God! Is it understood, Margot?" Ordered Roberts, as heatedly reacted; but is trying to hide his humiliation.

"Not a hair? Are you out of your mind, Nicolas? If so, I'll shave my head. That you can speak in their sermons. I don't want to live in our Church, in which stay deprived!" Happened be Magdalena's reaction.

"Dear sister, my decision isn't your business. It's crucial to have him here! Your selfish reason it's nothing for you to gain, or to loose? Sadly each profession has its risk. If I was a nurse, I'd go exhort those dying, Margot!" Changed the course of conversation Roberts.

Following he's listened to her opinion. Nicolas has shown unexpected stubbornness, and wouldn't change his mind.

Luckily Aaron has remained in this Church on the priest invitation.

In step with religious traditions, Roberts and Margot have decided to baptize young Dalton, in given him a name Uriel, formerly known Aaron. During his baptism, this priest's wore a silver belt with the Cross-hang that was a gift, in which he was baptized.

A Cross-hang from Aaron's neck, and inside seen a silver amulet, which he has inherited from his late parents.

For so-called Xiang Bo's, the Parish meant a place staying, packed with food. Be pleased, Aaron said with gratitude to Nicolas: "I don't want to leave!"

Days later, Roberts called on Aaron to come see him in the office-chamber. The priest's met him civilly in the lobby, and led Aaron to his office.

Once they have barged in, Aaron sat in a chair, while seen Roberts is walking around the room back and forth. He does a sudden stopover, is begun talking to Aaron.

The priest offers Aaron a Holy Bible, points to a certain page in this book: "Read this passage, you'll understand, ex-Cecil, now Uriel!"

"But why I should be called Uriel?" Aaron's become interested in the story of the name that he was given.

"Uriel has listed as the Fourth Angel in the Christian Gnostic (under this name),'- began reading Aaron: 'And he was carried John and his mother Saint Elizabeth when had to join the Holy Family after their flight... Uriel was commemorated together with the other Archangels and Angels, such as Gabriel...' Nicolas interrupts. Aaron's looked and grasped.

Now Nicolas is reciting: "Whilst Uriel flight was something memorable,"- this priest off talking, as if worried; and is enhanced: "Well, Uriel, how you're absorbing altogether?"

"By faith, you choose my new name,"- humbly, but caustic, responded Aaron.

The priest would flare up, but restrained himself: "Share your feet to me!" Has ordered Roberts. Once he is inclined, and grunting; Roberts then begun examining: "Legs like legs? Nothing unusual, or not?"

On the soles are no springs, vehicles. "Forgive me, haven't you been taught by Buddhist Monks levitating?"

Then he asked: "Though I've claimed that levitation idle, which fancies sluggish tourists. Today it's easy to believe in miracles?" He halts; then is ongoing:

'Yet it could only be a clever trick, of a miracle in the Christian God?"

"I don't know what levitation is…" Cautiously responded Aaron.

The priest has jumped in the conversation, and said: "Well, if you are not lying to me, it meant you were cheating the God? And He will punish you by sending leprosy. But if you do said the truth, then if you wish to serve Him? He'll help you!"

"My whole life belongs to God who does miracles." Aaron has predicted.

"Go on, and carry the name of Uriel!" Directed him Roberts.

Aaron has long considered plan of his own. He's by now settled Himalayas area, then vaguely guessed: 'What awaits for me in the future, after they've turned me into a flying man?'

Apparently he craved for a miracle to strengthen faith and Religion. But why he didn't use this role to their advantage?

It was crucial for Aaron finding shelter, get to know people, and watch his back. Perhaps to collect money from them, as the Flying man?"

Despite him been naïve, he has to start independent life. More plans of what he ought to do, or where to go remained unclear? They often changed, are having invariably involved remarkably: Wu Lan, Song Chuan and little Yuan Lu.

The night has loomed over Chinese towns. Aaron saw a high-pitched tower, where people would plan the first step in a society ripe with him.

For the time being, in the Church, Aaron has felt hostility from Magdalena. She would avoid meeting him, and has barely responded to his bows and conversation.

On many occasions Magdalena so-called 'a missionary Sister in a skirt', has patronized Aaron, called Uriel, as often as she possible could.

Then one evening the priest Roberts has a long conversation with those boys from the Church.

Be resilient to his sister, the priest wouldn't invite Uriel in the office, and climbed into his chamber that happened be an attic room, where he lived solitary.

In meantime, Aaron was extremely modest in taken food for days, with no ending would be poring over the Bible. Besides he's singing with the Gospel choir.

The zeal and a rapid progress Aaron called Uriel, with this the priest was pleased and impressed, and he had no idea that his pupil studied the history of religions and almost all the topics taught in the Monastery.

In time, Aaron was solemnly baptized, and being given a new name Uriel, in Abbreviated Ritual of the priest and his sister, Magdalena that have called him.

Meanwhile, Aaron was living and aided by the priest with no reliance; but strengthened from Margot that almost 'put him to the coffin' with her mentor.

Chapter 20

THEN once upon Sunday a 'miracle' has happened. A minute ago, seen Roberts in a half-empty Church, where he's preached a Sermon of Faith, or miracles of divine intervention, in the human affairs: "God almighty, as if it doesn't come to us, people in need! It is only because you're all having not sufficient faith asking Him about it. To prove once and for all, I say to you, it's written in Scriptures, if 'ye' have faith as a grain of mustard seed. 'Ye' shall say into the mountain! Move from here up to there and it will move; but nothing shall be impossible for you."

Aaron called Uriel, meanwhile be seated on the first bench. By hearing these words, he suddenly comes in the midst of the Church, squeezed prayer, looks to the sky: "I believe God, Thou hast done for my faith! Raise me!"

Unforeseen a young man's body has wavered, and elevated to the ceiling, his legs are three feet away from the floor. See those visitors became so wild, after start noises, are doing in high-pitched, as one: "A miracle! God send us an Angel!"

Uriel has still hung in the air for a while; ensuing he is plunged slowly down.

"Thank you, God for that miracle!" Declared the priest Roberts. To amass even more invitees, Roberts gripped the lectern of the realm, to keep him from a fall, and he's turned pale, while his lower jaw trembling.

Suddenly, it's become silent in the Church, so that one and all could hear the fleas flying across. Those locals were seemed scared-stiff.

Aaron called Uriel has felt rather unimaginable, when he's elevated. Walls shook with hysterical, frenzied of the people's screams; the audience jumped up from their seats.

Many followers in the Church remained in panic, crying, and rushed to the door, crushing each other, while others are hurrying to touch Uriel. Many visitors that are seated, fell down to their knees, stretched out arms to him, others beat their breasts: laughing and crying; exclaiming: "It is God, who has sent us this Angel! He's from God! Yes, He is!" Have cried that public.

'If Fiend or Evildoer saw the situation, which occurred? No wonder he and London Center, would have pinned to The Flying Man with such hopes?' Aaron elevates, is smiling sheepishly, it looks as if he hasn't realized what happened?

The priest on a whim lifts up his right hand, as if is trying to restore order.

But he's shocked by latest development no less than others, and frantically been waving a hand.

It's resulted he slipped from the chair - legs didn't hold him. Roberts on the spot is shaken by this miracle, cause be out of breath; seen he sat down on a step of the podium.

More often than not, wearing a brown monk robe round her head a black shoal, Margot would hike few miles during a morning walk. She was wandering across the fields at this early morning of Sunday when people praying in Church, and listened to the Sermon of her brother, the priest.

Willful and capricious Magdalena's arrogance has brought a lot of troubles for Roberts, who called her seldom by her real name Margot. She hated farming, was fond of hunting horse riding; being clever presenting her photos in the circle of photographers. Margot mocked philanthropy, of which she said unpleasant things.

Quoting the shudder of her brother that for instance, was stating: among all the Greek philosophers, he favored Plato and Aristotle. Those two last were the crude materialists, and have proved that the soul and body was a match. She contrary, hated to remain in China, and has craved returning to Britain.

To maintain peace between everyone, the priest's explained with quirks to his stubborn sister: only encouragement of European influence would invigorate those local Chinese.

Seem mainland with tropical climate in this part of China often made an impact, so she needs to be tolerant: "Margot, you've to dispose all of this nonsense,"- tried to reassure her brother, the priest.

"But if you weren't my sister, I would fire you. Spurred the pigs, and look at this young man, Uriel with a possibility. Yes, I allowed him living in our Parish to strengthen faith of the Christ, which, apparently, requires implementation of all the dirty work. Perhaps, for development of Christian spirit over modesty and obedience!"

Depriving, which were not ever over, seen those persons collapsing in Church, blaring, and waving their hands in the air, whenever Aaron would uplift.

It's happened Sunday, reining in her gumboots, Margot was feeding the pigs; yet begun yelling at Aaron, and has called him: 'Wanderer!' Like she would call a dog.

She believed that 'this monkey', wasn't worthy to bear the name of Aaron:

"Didn't you hear, me, wanderer?"

Aaron in the meantime has made a shortcut, come within reach of her.

"Hey, you, what's happening?" She's asked him, pointing a whip to the Church.

"Well, in there, were effected people, Miss…" Responded Aaron.

She interrupts him: "Sister Magdalena to you!" Impatiently has swayed her whip, above Aaron's head.

He at once puts himself together, saying: "Xiang Bo, I mean Uriel, sister! I've jumped into the air, miss, and everyone were very scared,"- blurted out Aaron.

"Don't talk nonsense, Uriel! However…" Reacted Magdalena.

Aaron interrupts her: "Miss! I mean sister! That's,"- he's started to bounce. "It has a very clever left. 'As if Aaron stood on invisible bench'!"

Aaron jumped back, is trying to keep away from a whip that Margot whizzed with on him.

Based on the shoulder Felton, who's served in the Church, staggered out. Following Roberts come out.

"Minister, what's happened? I'm not welcome here?" Aaron asked; this has alarmed Magdalena. Despite she loved her brother, but in the soul of a little annoyed at his weakness of Aaron's appeal.

Roberts is walking toward the parish beside Aaron, near saw Margot horse riding; bending she's patting with a whip on horse's neck. Roberts's focused on him: "My child, tell me what's happened?"

"I need time to recover, reverend, and the best way to know what's made in the name of God? Is going to Church!" Aaron low-voiced to guard himself.

"In that case, stay as long as you need," - pathetically said Roberts.

Arriving in hamlet, having unfriendly glance at clipped the tail of a horse, Margot snapped at Aaron with a whip held above; and she yelled: "Wanderer, you a little devil!" Then she dismounted a horse.

Aaron really has looked like a drifter, when run out of the kitchen with a towel in his right hand.

"Take these pigs in the barns!" The nun ordered; laid back, she is straightening folds on her amazons.

"There you go, sister Magdalena. At least I know what this is? Have you been crying, Margot? What is it?"

Asked with concern Nicolas; and came within reach of her: 'I hope its tears of joy, Margot? Lord has allowed me to see a miracle!' Roberts said spontaneously.

She on a whim reacted, is in a biting wit: "Chin-chin! And this is the jumping-Uriel? You're calling him a miracle? On the contrary! Jesus was a miracle!" Margot frowned; even has become a little pale.

"Don't say that! God will punish you! Don't you see it fell in our lap? Cecil or Uriel is a great Saint!" He's reacted.

Priest doesn't jump of joy; contrary, he takes off: "Everyone saw it. God has done a miracle for his great faith." Alleged Roberts: "I always expect from you nothing-more than support!" He's said with yearn.

Spur-of-the-moment, she became fanatical: "That bodes well it will not lead, not once, I think. 'Atheist'!"

"Indignantly cried the old maid, and is humbly added - 'Judge not, and you not be judged'! May God forgive you be a sinner, and God's mercy, me!" Roberts reacted unkindly.

After Magdalena moved to the house rear of the Church, is thinking. On the way she stopover, is standing in front of garden's track.

Suddenly a crowd approached the house, is blaring: "Holy, Uriel! Bless him and God!" Next one voice cried: "Touch my son, and heal him! Let us touch your feet, Uriel,"- heard voices coming from the crowd.

Do not short of few tens of feet to the fence: they're farmers stopped; but wouldn't dare approach a place within the Church.

Surprisingly from the crowd came out Aaron called Uriel. The Chinese peasants carried their curtsies and moved back; heard they're talking excitedly. Head down, Uriel entered the garden, is going directly to the porch.

"Hey, Uriel, how did you get in there?" Sudden he's thought interrupted Margot.

Standing Aaron is having a word: "Why you think abysmal of the Church?"

Be unnoticed Wang Chou-Roberts, imposed: "If strongly trust nothing is impossible for Mankind, such is power of God!"

"I was faithfully praying to Lord to help me get up off the floor! And God has listened to me. It's true! Reverent, you picked up God alone, under the mouse or hair?" Aaron is tongue-tied, realizing said inappropriate.

Magdalena's smirked, seen her nostrils are extending, as she yelled: "Nonsense! I don't believe it? Well, the work's done in front of me by this trick, if you don't want me to call you a liar, Uriel?"

Aaron sighed, looked at the gate, on a bed of carnations and easily set foot on the head of a flower, which is not even bent.

Aaron went over heads of flowerbed, but stops short on the track; modestly watched her, and he is stating:

"He's made a funny trick?" Magdalena said to Nicolas; and is trying to hide her humiliation.

The next day Margo started the same discussion: 'Don't imagine you have convinced me of God's gift to you do miracles, Uriel?'

"I just did what you needed from me." Humbly reacted Aaron.

"So, picture perfect. And how do you think you used these tricks?" Has probed Margo.

"God will have shown me the way!" Responded Aaron called Uriel.

Margo stamped her foot frontward: "I hate hypocrisy!" She reviled. Resulting she is boldly: "Let's say you somehow manage to do it. It's not hypnosis. Well, then what this is? Are you going to do these same tricks only to plunge for hysterical women and old men in the Church? Either as a surprise simple for the girls, trembling by flowerbeds, like butterfly? Or, perhaps, you're going to get coinages at the Fairs? A human should be engaged in real man's job?"

Be unseen Wang Chou or Roberts approached; and said: 'If I were in your shoes, Margo, I'd admit to the fire. Or to save people from burning buildings, soaring on high floor, this doesn't reach fire escape. Would it work saving the community on the water, and not be portrayed a miracle worker? Yes, Uriel's the spirit!"

"God wouldn't have lived in wilderness on foreign bread. Maybe I will?" Appealed Uriel; has bowed his body down. He turns, and went in the room within Church.

"A clever rascal!" Claimed Margot, this's meant for Aaron. Synchronously she is begun observing the flowers.

Once Aaron called Uriel's absent, the priest said: "Margot, the die is cast. Uriel what is may! It's still the best way for timeout.

'I admit we must use Uriel, no matter what he's signifying. And converted to Christianity by the mass of gentiles? But to draw up a brilliant report and leave for Britain with the glory that I'm a great priest. Esteem me, allow my successor to cut it with all I discerned?"

Yet Nicolas has dreamed receiving awards from metropolitan board of the University, or perhaps even under the guidance of Bishopric.

The study reigned by Magdalena; she's run, waving newspapers in her hand, then suddenly yelled: "Minister, I think that your Cecil has constantly deceived us! Here, read the newspapers all they talk about is the Flying man! This, of course, was related to Xiang Bo, or what's his name is?"

"Have news reported that the flying man was in-the-air always?" Asked her this priest.

"Yes. He isn't a fake, for the reason that a pilot in-midair saw him flying. And the beetles airborne; don't believe he's a miracle!" Margo is intensely. Still handed him newspapers.

To her allegations about Aaron, Roberts trusted: "Margot! If you wish quickly return to London, don't show anyone the newspapers! If it comes to the spotlight, this will resolve for big scandal? And, don't tell about Cecil, who's real name is Aaron. My main concern is you: don't interfere in whatever involves me. I beg you..." He put hands like is praying. "This problem will last only a few weeks.

'I'm given you my word, then we can go to England permanently!" Decided Roberts.

Although Aaron was neither aware of their conversation; nor has found the article in nun's closet about him.

So far summon of devotion, she's craved going down smoothly from brother's office; but Margo has fallen, bruised her knees; then chided herself in a lack of faith, and went to the murky chamber.

News of the miracle in the Church has spread throughout surrounds: 'You would have thought that Uriel caused local Chinese become crazy?'

Magdalena sprang all along... As the nun closed her eyes, and glared them into pots or scissors, she then hissed: "Get up! Get up! I believe."

While, near the kitchen, Aaron jumped, trying in vain getting up into the air, is shouting: "I believe! Hop... Little Faith. And yet, I believe! Hop! Yes, it's increased faith! We all should believe in God! Hop..."

Time was flying quickly; rumors have it that in neighboring villages those Chinese locals were jumping from the roof, trying to walk on water, or would fanatically cry: "I believe in our Lord! God is great!" Hurt of those, stuck in the mud...

Unpredictably, Nicolas decided traveling with Uriel to other Churches, remote to perform sermon of blessing to local Chinese.

One of sacred-rituals in a village, Aaron elevated to the ceiling, looking down to the public; surprisingly he's eyes caught Wu Lan, standing, and is watching him gloriously.

'He is an Angel God send us from Heaven!' Proclaimed priest. Marvel of success surpassed all Aaron's expectations.

Without thinking of the consequences, Aaron promptly, began tumbling, and like an arrow, flew toward her. Descending close to her ear, he has whispered: "There's no the time to talk. I'll come to see you, later! Wait for me outskirts of the village. I'll come by night."

At night Aaron landed outskirts of hamlet, where a garden of flowers was enchanting people.

There came into view Wu Lan, in a flash has approached outskirts of the village. She is anxiously observing the sky, waiting for Aaron's return.

Soon Wu Lan has noticed him flying, and is become excited. Aaron too saw her, and directly began landing nearby her standing.

In next to no time they moved to a shelter, and have seated down. Aaron breaks silence: "'Oh, Wu Lan, I didn't dream to see you here? It's been so long since we met?"

She curtsies her head down modestly: "Yes, Sky Lord, I was looking for you, and finally heard that you were here! It's safe for you?"

There he is talking to this girl: 'Wu Lan, I've it under control!'

Despite Aaron is keen to speak with Wu Lan, but he doesn't forget of danger; and in a risky situation both have found themselves in.

Instinctively he is low voicing: "Wu Lan! What you're doing in this region? And why you in that Church?"

She's kept her head down; and is low voicing: 'I'm happy to see you, Sky Lord! Wait, I'll tell all. I went to find if you where in Buddhist Temple?' She stops talking; is taken deep breaths; and ongoing: "Besides, two traditional days, the fifth day of the fourth month together with fifteenth day of the tenth month of each Tibetan year is celebrated with singing and dancing in Wencheng's honor. I was the luckiest; there choose me among other women performing in honor of Princess Wencheng." Wu Lan took a deep breath; and tells more of her story: "I heard that our women's choir would perform in auditorium. Going there, some of us were selected to be dancers. I sang with a high pitch voice... It's about how I become Princess that Buddha would have chosen, and the rest is history!" She stops; looks at him, then prolongs: "There were Monks of High Rank asked if I wish to become a singer and dancer in the choir? I've rehearsed to sing and dance, before. The board of adjudicators has accepted me, and I've easily performed, as Princess.

'In respect they've invited me here; my aim was to see you. Now we're equal, Sky Lord!" She's discontinued, her eyes with sadness.

He seems be concerned, when interrupts her; is said alone: "Wu Lan, I'm glad that we've met at last. I didn't expect to find you here. How's your dad?"

"After my mother died, he has fallen sick..."

Aaron interrupts her: "You shouldn't leave your dad alone, God knows what could happen to him? You've to return home! Give my respect to him!"

Their meeting extend close to midnight; easygoing they're following their feelings; as hooked on, evolving intimate for them alone, as this pair of 'loving birds' began passionately kissing.

Realizing both equally ripe for love, resulting: they're getting undressed steadfast.

Going with the flow, they look excited. Remarkably Aaron declares: 'I fell in love with you, girl!'

She is staring at him lovingly; behaving very much keenly: 'I love you more, Sky Lord!'

A full moon sparkled, got past the window. Arising Aaron and Wu Lan are sliding over the hay, …passionate kissing with cuddles, like they've a love fever.

Following of love making amidst those young adults is evolving...

In the barn lovemaking intuitively has developed between a pair of loving birds. This was the first time of an erotic experience for both of them making love.

The next day, developed amazing cockcrow that bathed in sunlight. In this part of China, it appears a pond from, where hot water spring slides down the Mountains.

Perceived trembling voices with splashes, like they're with love fever. It's surfaced foggy alfresco; where a waterfall cascading, and silhouettes of two come into view are staying in a pool of water. There are viewing haze images of Wu Lan and Aaron passionately kissing in this pond.

Awhile after, Aaron seems be troubled, its crucial that she accepts his strategy.

'Why you need to leave, darling? Is it part of your plan for disperse that will happen soon?' Attentively has asked Wu Lan.

"Partly. Do you, accept my idea, Wu Lan?" Asked Aaron. She converts to silence; and thought for a moment.

Wu Lan's look with admiration for Aaron, she's enlightened of her view: "Yes!"

Later on, those lovebirds are out of the pond. Downhill Wu Lan entered a set up space inside the tent, is wearing a robe over that covered her slim-body. By way of observing her figure, Aaron changes to modesty; has budged with his shoulders.

Soon both put their heads together. Aaron smiles, is fond of happiness are shared by both of them; this has virtually replaced his nightmares. Intuitively Aaron is staring at Wu Lan, he's feelings have reflected in his eyes. She equally is watching him fondly, this's developing into love making between those two lovebirds.

"I've to leave soon,"- Wu Lan's whispered into his earlobe.

"I need to go too. Will you wait for me, Wu Lan?" Aaron's asked desperately.

"Yes, I'll wait, Sky Lord!" She said with beam, and her face lit up.

Meanwhile, every day Aaron's performed Sacred Amenity, in the Church that accommodated those, who would arrive from nowhere, until now: it's stayed half empty.

This priest has evangelized eloquent on the power of faith, with influence of Christian God, and has gained a direct advantage over 'pagan' of Gods.

Early enough Roberts converted to Christianity hundreds of his followers of Chinese origin. Report has grown and it shed light, and yet, in the congregation those locals listened gracefully to Sermon, but the priest wasn't careful.

Every Sunday at Church's Services, one and all were eagerly awaiting entrance of the miracle worker, Uriel, who habitually would appear after each Sermon; and elevating before the astonished audience. His adjustment bothered the priest with issues 'to acquire the Faith'.

Rapidly, by which works wonder why no one else is doing it? Except for Aaron more often than not it was a cover-up.

In the meantime, the priest explained as best he could, has called for fortitude that was given advice to local Chinese, and making sort of guide strengthening the faith.

Rumors have it that those locals remembered prayers, which meaning they didn't understand. And their dreams of what wonders have been done once they begin possess the faith.

It must be said that margin of those locals didn't dream nor about relocation to the mountains, or to stop the sun? Only about to have a new home, feeding pigs, consuming of a daily handful of rice, healing diseases, and none of 'The Kingdom of Heaven'.

At the sessions existing of Heaven, which having endured beyond the walls of the Church but couldn't accommodate all the newcomers; and it's begun showing for the Europeans.

First the local Chinese men among others of the King Ming Dynasty, and between those visitors that were foreigners.

Luckily, no one be even the faith of a mustard seed, or the omnipotence of the Holy faith that was a hoax about what being talking loudly on most affected. The time must not be lost, and it 'doesn't wait for men, or women?'

Randomly one day the priest has stunned the community with a message of forthcoming Festive prayer service at Church's door; on the occasion of arisen miracles of a talented man came from the Sky... all been dedicated to Uriel.

Chapter 21

MANY days have passed. A minute ago it's appeared a violet twilight has covered metropolis through with gray clouds by, which formed circle around.

Here came into view a hotel-room in China, where be held a meeting by two Americans, who become known Jimmy Brandton, is reading an article. He's handed magazine laughingly to a second man, named Glen Chatelaine appears be seated on other side of the room. Both are roughly in the age of their late twenties, or early thirties, medium-tall; Glen is ash-blond; has gray-hazel eyed, with a medium hairstyle. Jimmy has dark eyes, and black hair medium-short haircut.

Promptly Glen began talking: 'Brandton, here are the wonders of China! Look, what kind of nonsense they wrote in their local papers? Obviously, the Chinese public is more trusting than the Americans, but not stupid. In magazine, they dare to claim that the Flying man is existed. But feasibly avoid, journalists point of view about, what kind of person he, is?'

Now Jimmy is begun reading the article; then expressed his opinion wisely: "It would-be good if we can get this flying man in our Circus troupe?"

Glen began laughing, and vocally approves: "You bet!"

But Brandton seems be thoughtful: "I'm quite serious, Glen! On one occasion I have spoken to someone among our Chinese recruiters, about this Flying man, and many of these staffs insisted that story wasn't a myth. And yet, none of them saw him." He becomes quiet, and takes a breath; then puts in the picture: "Tamer of snakes...

'I cannot recall the man's name, but he has insisted that saw with his own eyes, the Flying man, who's young.

'It had occurred when he stole a girl and a boy on a Sunday Fair. Later he flew away with both children, to God knows where?"

Glen has begun shaken his head, as if is doubted. And yet, soon he came to believe in the existence of the Flying man.

Brandton has spoken previously with those, who witnessed the Flying man, before Jimmy and Glen approached the area…

One among the locals happens thrilled, telling about: "I saw the Flying Man, or rather anew Angel in the Sky, with my own eyes!" He halts of talking; and is indicating to the door: "I can point to you the area, where he is…"

Glen looks serious; and become interested in finding the flying man: "Okay, let's change the route, and drive to find this Flying man?"

That meeting has taken place, on the way to, where a Circus tent was set up. Glen and Jimmy have met those en route, who retuned from the Church.

Walking out of the Church, Roberts has noticed two strangers with an American accent, struck him by an exceptional interest they indicated toward Aaron, called Uriel.

In the meantime, Roberts in Church's chamber cautiously thought, before talking to Aaron.

Besides his concern wasn't in vain: 'I'm almost certain those men were reporters? Yet, they can spoil the whole thing for me?'

The next morning, those two American men came to meet Aaron Xiang Bo called Uriel. Not paying any attention to noises around, they're coming from a crowd, and focused on Uriel.

Jimmy directly began interaction with Aaron: "Excuse us, young man, can you, spear a moment speak to us in private, please? It's taken us a lot to find you."

"At your service, fellows! What can I do for you?" To keep on, they went out with those from a crowd, toward waiting on the road, other than for American cars.

Glen bravely began talking-to Aaron: "We tried to meet you for a long time. And we want to know more about your life, Mister?"

Aaron without a second thought jumps in: "I'm Uriel! What do you've in mind?"

Jimmy came straight to the point: "We believe that you're the Flying man?"

Uriel is frank, but tense: "What if I'm flying man! How it concerns you're?"

The clever Americans look at each-other is admired Aaron. Then Glen declared: "Let's cut to the chaise, we here with a business proposition, Uriel," he stops talking,

When the conversation was over, Aaron said goodbye to those two, one of them opened car door, and they have vanished inside.

Roberts, meantime, saw those two men sat in the car; but he didn't walk away, instead began considering.

Minutes later, the priest's questioned Aaron called Uriel, in the attic where was his lodging: "Who those men, you were talking to, my son?"

"You mean I spoke with two newcomers, reverend?" Has played a fool Aaron.

"Yes, two men. What were you're discussing?" He doesn't let it go, looks as if is jealous being governed by his sister.

"They were interested in me be the Flying man!" Aaron's in hesitated voice.

On this occasion he exposed cloak-and-dagger: "You know who I'm? I've to be honest, because soon I must leave. I'm grateful to you minister, for accepting me. And thanks you, sir, for the shelter and hospitality, you've given me!"

After those Americans left, Nicolas has thought: "The main thing for me was get respected by local Chinese. Soon Aaron will leave. It's a good thing he's disappearing? It's less risk."

The next day, at late afternoon Glen and Jimmy came to see Aaron called Uriel again, it appears they've visited Roberts's Church.

They're not timid when approached him; and have begun their discussion with Aaron plainspoken: "Excuse me, can we speak-up with you in privative?"

At first, Glen talked with Aaron briefly in their car; its effect was appropriate for both parties.

Days later, Glen and Jimmy are having come within reach of so-called Uriel. He stood at the scene in a edifice, which was part of the Church, getting ready for his performance, as an 'Angel'...

Despite tough negotiations between those, both Americans have got a chance struck a deal with Aaron. However, they struggled to talk him into signing a contract, on the spot.

Practical Americans weren't interested, where his family originated from; or Uriel's character stands for; either what Aaron's past was? Only they want it is 'The Flying man' working for them.

Jimmy inclined his head toward the exit, as a hint to Glen, then is uttering: "Glen, listen, if he is an Angel, then I'm a disembodied spirit? Ha-ha-ha!"

Seem Glen wasn't amazed; without a moment of hesitation, he returns to strike a deal with Aaron; in that case he'd have answered: "Well, you right, young man! I want to make you an offer. What are your conditions?"

Jimmy doesn't look shocked from witnessing Aaron elevating, be ready to support Glen negotiation with him: "Nice seeing you again, Uriel! Let's talk business, we interested in the phenomenon you can perform, which is flying! Do you want to work for us? We'll fly you to America, you should get great rewards working there!"

Spur-of-the-moment, Aaron's taken mouthful of air. He is having a minute to consider: "I know America is far from China. To stay abroad it'll be safe for me, over there?"

Jimmy, in the meantime, turns to Glen, and talks quietly: "We must get him to work for us, on his own accord. Destiny came to meet us with him?"

Shortly after, Aaron without thinking twice, has agreed. Though his reaction has utterly puzzled Glen Chatelaine, but not Jimmy Brandton.

"Both of us don't deal with Angels or Demons, whether you want us to believe in it or not? Mister Uriel, do you agree working for our Circus?"

Aaron's become interested, and is responding: "Yes, I agree to work for you! And I'm not an Angel!"

Glen raises his right hand, as if has indicated: "I believe you! But don't bargain with us! As the French say, 'sans pair' has no equal. And yet, you either an Angel, or an idiot, for the criminals who want to get away across the sea, will catch a lot of cash out of you."

Jimmy comes to a point: "This is not the place to discuss, come later to our hotel, we'll talk further there. It's settled, Uriel?"

Meantime, resulting Roberts's said since was allowed: "Well then, Uriel, you a free man, and can go anywhere you like, even with them. And when do you plan leaving?"

Aaron without thinking is responded: "Possibly in few days time. If you find it's necessary for me staying longer here, and do performance on last miracle?"

"No! Go-on, then, my boy," has alleged Roberts with a fault kindness to Aaron.

Soon Roberts hurried to tell Church staffs of the latest news: "Uriel is leaving!"

At the same day, in the evening, Jimmy touched upon issue of the Flying man. Be expert dealing with the Celebrities, Jimmy's thought of Uriel's past, said: "I guess, this young man knows, neither real life, nor how he can make money?"

This kind of suggestion lifted up Glen's mood: "Well then, on the terms that will satisfy us, we must talk about it?"

Jimmy breaks in, fearing the Circus boss couldn't convince that the flying man has brought the idea; knowing Uriel is the only one in the world.

On that night, saw Aaron has arrived in their hotel-room, but seems be uneasy: "Fellows, I would like to ask you only for…"

Jimmy waved at this point his right hand in the air: "About the payment, if we cannot agree, it's always a collusion?"

Aaron called Uriel, responded: "No! It's not that."

The Americans are attentive. Promptly Glen intrudes; and is asking: "What would you like us to do, Uriel? Just tell us? We'll see if we can be of assistance?"

Aaron is looking humbly: "Before we travel abroad, first I need to visit a place to see my good friends, and another person who's dear to me. I'll need your help after all?"

Despite the Americans take-a-back when look at one another; and are reflecting on.

Glen decided: is coming up with a solution; and tells him so: "Of course, mister Uriel, we're at your service, any time!"

It's passed an hour since Aaron left; those Americans were stayed in the hotel-room to reflect on.

Glen began analyzing the situation. And without more ado, he is asking Jimmy: "Brandton, what do you think of him?"

Brandton without hesitation vents his point of view: "I say, we've found a 'golden-goose' for your old man, and for the Trust - it's Uriel. As you can see, China is the country of miracles, without doubt!" He suddenly shushes; and points his finger toward a poster: "And I'll take care of advertising!"

Advertising was Jimmy's favorite hobbyhorse. Now he thinks for a jiffy on the go, and tells more: "The pastor has found Uriel early enough. However, we came up with a more brilliant idea. And we play for the benefit of the pastor, to our interests?" Brandton silenced for a tick. Next he unveils the idea: "Why don't we use Uriel tricks to promote our advertising? Let him rise to a height over eighty feet. After all, we have bought the Flying man?"

Glen produced a vogue smile; then is declaring: "Uriel will praise the Sky in our Circus!"

Brandton's shaken his head, as if is disagreed: "I object, for a reason that I'm finding ventures a little practical, even insensitive!"

On a whim, the stubborn Chatelaine insisted, and Brandton having to give in to his demand. Now Glen waves a hand in the air, as if has won: "I'm dreaming how we'll demonstrate to America the Flying man?" He clams up with thrill; suddenly Glen takes out of his pocket piece of paper.

Glen meantime, moves his head to the door, has affirmed: 'Now we have to go, I want to send a message to inform of the arrival in America of the Flying man: a world miracle is coming! How's this for Advertising, Jimmy?'

Chapter 22

MANY days have passed since; then one evening, in the fires of sunset, gold-domed marble, where it's been revealed a bulky Lee Pong mentioned around.

Aaron was seated in the car; Glen and Jimmy have driven swapping places while steering the wheel in the evening.

Aaron is seemingly into remembering: "I see a sight of the palace, and my heart is pounding. After all, Wu Lan's fate is most interest me!"

Passing by familiar edifices, Aaron looked at the verandas; is ongoing: 'There looks to me amongst them Wu Lan? Or it's could be another woman, looked like her? Here I can fly from the car to that balcony in one minute? But I've made a promise to Glen not to fly?' Aaron on the spot has resisted temptation.

The next morning, from a distance shows up an auto, where interior sees the two Americans and Aaron; driving, were moving toward somebody's shed.

Aaron, meanwhile, points a hand from the car-window to show his bosses: "Look over there, fellows, that's the Lake, and the grove. Here it is, Wu Tang's shed!"

After Aaron's got out of the car, and from a distance seen: Song Chuan and Wu Lan are stand-up of their seats, while this girl Yuan Lu sitting near them.

Aaron's exaggerated with excitement; and takes off, runs a half-a-mile...

Unable to contain his happiness, he ran, barely touched the ground with underfoot, then Aaron is elevating, and begun flying without realizing.

To not interfere with his rendezvous, Brandton instructs the driver: "Drive towards the apple trees, and stop there, please!"

Seen this drawing, Jimmy clarifies to Glen: "Look how he runs? We will do a world great sprinter out of him."

In the meantime, Wu Lan sits alongside Song Chuan and Yuan Lu, saw on the steps of a porch, at the sight where Aaron is approaching, they erected and guessing; but none of the three recognized him.

Aaron takes a chance, and jumps in: "Can you recall, Song Chuan, how once I tore apples for you and for little Yuan Lu?"

Something has struck Song Chuan; he began shouting: "Is it really you, brother Bo?"

The boy promptly has rushed to meet his friend; due to be confused, he does stop: seen Aaron is wearing an elegant piece of suit, with a cap; and his hair cut short.

Aaron began laughing with joy: "Yes it's me, Song Chuan! How you're doing, my friend?"- Next he hugged this boy, who has clung to his arm.

Once Wu Lan has learned that it was 'Sky Lord', she bowed to the ground, and kissed his legs.

But Glen thinks: "Then again, before Aaron was this 'wall of worship'?"

Aaron instead, craved to hug Wu Lan, and whispered: "I love you, Wu Lan! And I want you to become my wife?"

Except her curtsy tied his movements: "Sorry, it's not the right time and place, yet!" She said.

Spur-of-the-moment Aaron comes within reach of Wu Lan; it seems he's humbled, when is said inappropriately: "Wu Lan! You see I've fulfilled my promise? Did you wait on me?"

Her answer confused him: "No, Sky Lord, but I've got a vision that we'll meet!" She became silent; her head in curtsy, as if is embarrassed.

Aaron's tongue-tied. Resulting he turns to look around: "I came to you, Wu Lan. But, where is mister Wu Tang?"

She looks with enthusiasm at Aaron; then her expression changed to sad: "We've bad news, Sky Lord. My mom's death took its toll, and distressed my father the most. It has caused him fallen sick."

Without losing a minute, Aaron swiftly entered Wu Tang's shed. Inside appears a dark room, whereas he saw Wu Tang, who's laid in bed, looking white as a stone.

Aaron came within reach of the old man's bed, and shook hands with him. Seeing Wu Tang's eyes have flashed with joy. Aaron bends; and is talking gently to this elderly Chinese man: "Mister Wu Tang, how you're feeling?"

Wu Tang has struggled to speak: "Is it you, God? Wu Lan was right, you couldn't die in that place? And you come to see me?

'Thank you, Sky Lord, for everything you've done for us!" The man takes a break; seems he is short of breath: "You see, Sky Lord, my long partner in life, my dear wife, had died. So, my death is near..."

Aaron takes the man's withered hand; and impulsively has interrupted him; tries to calm him down, meaning: "You will not die, sir!"

Received sound of Wu Tang's weak voice, as he's responded: "There's an old Chinese say 'All born beings must die. Dried flowers shouldn't overshadow the eyes when burnt them'!"

In a difficult situation, Aaron is kept calming down this man: "No, Mr. Wu Tang, you'll recover. I'll send doctors to treat you! And, mister Wu Tang, when you recover, we'll all go to America! You Wu Lan, Song Chuan and this girl that I brought with me, Yuan Lu. But I'm not a God, my name is Xian Wei, and I love Wu Lan. I want her to become my wife?"

Wu Tang closed his eyes. And is moving slowly in front of his hands, as if fending off him lost in own thoughts. This old man looks Aaron in the eyes; said with joy: 'Thank you, Xian Wei, for the highest honor known you! Wu Lan is concerned about my health, said she wouldn't marry anyone. From the time when you've left, she refused to marry Woe Ming. This young man was in despair, and soon after Woe Ming went to a big city to look for a job. He didn't return, ever since.'- He became silent; and takes a profound breath. This oldest is resumed talking: "If I shall die, what will happen to Wu Lan? But God wouldn't send her a husband, to protect her? There were suitors for her, though Wu Lan's impoverished girl, who may want her?"

Spur-of-the-moment Aaron raised his head, seems is prying, discovering of another man, who's in love with Wu Lan: all together has made him jealous.

Quickly Aaron's mood changed; and he is ardently protested: "God and Buddha would-be happy having for a wife Wu Lan! I know I'll!"

Wu Tang promptly opens his eyes, looks at Aaron, and gave a smile: "But, will the wife be happy in unequal marriage, with you, Sky Lord?"

Aaron seems is nervous with old man's morality. Impulsively he turns be hotly, to prove to Wu Tang the possibility of him and Wu Lan marriage: 'I hope so, sir! I cannot take your daughter with me? And I trust to leave with you the kids, Yuan Lu, and Song, mister Wu Tang!' Aaron became silent for a jiffy; but saw he is distressed. Next he's ongoing: "Well then, sir, we'll talk about."

Aaron rapidly gets of his sit; and walks off, heading for the porch.

Reaching the porch, he is approached Wu Lan; and taking her hands in his, said: "Wu Lan! I'll send a doctor to your father, and he will feel better. I forbid you: don't invite a sorcerer, he'll kill Wu Tang, like he's caused death to his own son!" Aaron halts talking; then became serious: "You're waiting for someone else, not for me, Wu Lan? I've to go, but I'll be back,'- intuitively Aaron hasn't taken eyes away from her pale face.

Wu Lan replied loudly: "No!"

Aaron seems is inspired, and declared: "When your dad gets well, I want you to become my wife? Then I will take all of you're with me,'- Aaron still looks in her eyes.

Although she isn't a girl anymore, but not a woman yet, seems be well-mannered.

But her expression of suffering, and fear, rather than joy caused Aaron a sharp pain in his heart: "Now I wish I can make you happy? Why you silent, Wu Lan?"

She in her turn is acting courteously: "I don't know what to say to you, Sky lord?"

Aaron seems is embarrassed, still is attracted: "Say, what comes to your mind? Do you love me, Wu Lan?"

"I love you, but..."- She's responded.

This young woman stood with downcast eyes; seen her hands have trembled in Aaron's hands.

Song Chuan jumped straight in the conversation: "Wu Lan was waiting for you all this time, brother Bo! All she talked about was you! Say we all will travel together, with you?"

Yet Aaron has interrupted him; then he turns around: "Wait, a minute, Song Chuan, I'll be right back!"

Aaron is walking away swiftly to the car that waited aside.

Approaching the vehicle, Aaron bows, puts his head inside car window; and is assumed: "Mister Chatelaine, my apology, but you've promised me money up-front?"

Instinctively Jimmy puts a hand in his pocket: "Uriel, I'll give you some money! How much do you need?"

Aaron accepted cash from Jimmy, and looking at the amount, he doesn't appear happy; that's why is reacting: "That's not enough, Mr. Brandton! Do you see my friends over there? In the shed is an elderly man, Mr. Wu Tang, who's very sick, he needs a doctor, and medication for his recovery!"

Resulting Glen puts a hand in his pocket, and insert a band with dollars. He then passes it to Aaron: "I'm giving you several hundred US dollars, but we must hurry to leave?"

Glen is of little interest in money; the main thing for him was to take Aaron away from China.

Even if there's a considerable amount, on the scale of the Circus Trusts as a good will offer to help a poor Chinese family it was nothing.

For Aaron, it was significant. With a sense of gratitude he promptly takes the money, still thought about: "How stupid I was, not to take the US Dollars before? And buy gifts for Mr. Wu Tang, and for all of them? They were so happy to see me! I'll send them more gifts from America."

Returning back to an old man shed, Aaron tells: "That's for you, mister Wu Tang! Take that charitable amount, please; it's for your health, and recovery!"

Resulting to be relieved to help; Aaron turns towards Wu Lan, and signifies: 'Make sure to call a doctor, as soon as possible, Wu Lan. Don't forget your father needs nutritious food to eat. Don't worry about money, I'll send you more. I'll be back for all of you're. Goodbye, Mr. Wu Tang, and get well soon!'

Wu Tang has produced a vogue smile, and whispered: "Thank you, young man! Take care, let God keep you safe, goodbye and good luck, Sky Lord!"

Once they've reached the porch, Aaron moves closer to Wu Lan, and boldly has kissed her on the lips. Seen her face instantly turn pink: "Good-bye my, Wu Lan! Take care of your father, Song Chuan, and Yuan Lu, and of course of yourself!

'I'll send you many parcels with gifts, and you've to write to me! I promise, I'll come back for you!"

Wu Lan looks, as if is in delirium; and said, kept staring into the space: "I will wait for you, Sky Lord! But dreams are come and go..."

Aaron is with a nervy smile, when looked at her, marveling: "It will not be a dream! It will work for us, darling! I'm asking you, please, wait for me, Wu Lan!"

Impulsively Song Chuan interrupts; and began pleading him: "Take me with you, brother Bo!"

Aaron clumsily is begun caressing his head; then he grabs boy's hand. Abruptly he's started walking with him toward sideways: "I'll be glad to take you with me, Song Chuan. Look, and think carefully! Now, it's very tough times for Wu Lan, being on her own, and taking care of her sick dad? It's all in your and Yuan Lu's hands, you both have to help her!"

This time around Song Chuan's resonated with Aaron: "Yes, it's true, brother Bo. We must wait until her father feels better, and recovers!"

Aaron nods his head, as if has decided: "Then you all will come to live with me! There's nothing I wouldn't do for all of you're!"

In next to no time Aaron has come back to the car, where his new boss and the executive are waiting for him.

Once car's ignition started with heavy feel, with those three are seated inside; the vehicle began moving fast.

Later that afternoon, Aaron seats in the interior of a car that drove him farther away from his friends. While, he is considering meticulously: "What has made me leave my friends behind? Why travel far away, to unknown country, to America?

'What waits for me there? It would be better for me to stay with my friends here? Since I could fly there again as a helpless person, playing on fate, for prey of the evil men? They might destroy my friends, and Wu Lan? No, I'm doing the right thing, do I?"

Yet, in his ears still have resonated Wu Lan's mysterious words: 'Dreams are coming and going. Everything would-be passing, like fantasy!'

Right this moment, in Monastery sees Evildoer or 'Master Guru', tongue in cheek, and is having intense talk with Fiend known as Wong Da.

Besides them in the room has appeared Spurt, known as Dr. Hui Wei.

Fiend's voice received been sarcastic: "And, who would this be, a ghost from the sky? Rumor has it that local Chinese call him Sky Lord?"

A sudden Spurt interrupts him: "Life itself is a miracle! My associate clued-up us, and I mean who will be the new Flying Man?"

On the spot, those two men are curious. But Evildoer alone is probed Spurt: "I'm intrigued, doctor, who would it be?"

Spurt gave a smirk; ensuing he gets up of his sit. As he's adjusted part of his jacket; and is revealing:

'I nominate myself, for I need this ability to fly. From the time when the experiments began, I have succeeded!

'I've decided creating more flying men, for allocation to Space City, where the people would be flying in and out!'

Resulting to prove impossibility to those Spurt jumps, but something goes wrong!

By his attempt has jumped to the ceiling; and fractured his skull... It's caused Spurt starts bleeding profusely, which emerged off his brain.

Shortly, Spurt has died in this Hospital, where he worked for years; still never regaining consciousness.

PART – IV
'THE SKY'S THE LIMIT'

Chapter 23

DAYTIME was flying like birds for Jimmy, Glen and Aaron. Days later, a trio boarded a plane, where they're hassled-free. Except Glen and Brandton stay in first class, but Aaron is seen in economy sits.

Years ago those Americans decided relocate their business to China. Now they're development have produced one of the oldest in North America that managed by the Circus Trust. Perceiving they're discussing matter of concern through a long flight, Aaron doesn't hear.

Seen Aaron is seated away in economy class; from the time when he walked and talked to his boss, Glen; and decided this is where he wanted to remain.

Jimmy is having a word to say, indignantly: "To deceit the public in our Circus with mind set? To this I object, it's absurd! Of course, the audience will watch the flying man!"

"Many people would-be lacking to observe his first flights without a plane, this can amass negativity? Then the public will quickly get used to great things. The spectators can pay big bucks for extraordinary Uriel!"- Be excited Glen.

"The same will happen with Uriel, as with other performers. Spectators would watch him once or twice, but for the third time they'll not come to our Circus?" Voiced his opinion Brandton.

Hearing of such honest account Glen's mood has changed been heated: "You wrong, Jimmy! We'd have time to amass those millions with Uriel's unique performance!"

This time, Brandton began objecting with sarcasm: "How we could amass millions?"

Glen interrupts him, is declaring: "Jimmy, don't be a pain in the ass! By sport!"

Jimmy shakes his head, be difficult: "Okay, Glen! Let's say you will make it happen? How you plan to use Uriel?"

Glen looks around, be vigilant; talks with confidence: 'Be quiet, Jimmy! First of all, you do remember: he is able to fly? Don't report it to our authorities! And, don't tell anyone? Understood? If the audiences will be bored, they would struggle over performance timeless, which is astonishing change of the terms, and grand finale in our Circus! And we'll deliver the best Show ever, for audience with the rarest animals in the world too,'- Glen clams up for a jiffy.

Next he proclaims: "For example they'll be ready to watch some silly cockfights for hours. Passions must sparkle on people's worry bettors!"

Brandton giggled, resulting he moves his head up and down: "Aha, I think it's sunk to me? Perhaps you right, Glen?" He became silent; and fixes into thinking.

Still, Glen is confident: "Yes, I'm right! With one hundred per cent, dude!"

At this point, Glen makes a grimace like is excited: "Trust me, we've found a priceless Star, someone like Uriel, it is already a success!"

Time flew quickly, since those three: Glen, Jimmy and Aaron called Uriel, have landed in America.

Before long, in office of the Circus, an old-looking man, happen be Glen's dad Chatelaine senior, seemed is content they discovered a new acrobat-juggler who's going to perform: "I'm awfully happy with your discovery in China, fellows! As for you, Jimmy your plans have fully endorsed by entire Board of the Circus Trust."

Brandton analogous, when shaped a smile, with a half bend, near him: 'Thank you, sir, but he isn't a juggler. I'd be glad to oblige you anytime, Mr. Chatelaine! Though you've to remember, no-one in America should know this young man we brought is Uriel, or Aaron, and he is The Flying Man!'

Chatelaine senior trifles, impulsively: "Whatever his name? The Flying man?"

Glen badges in, to protect his investment: "Do you realize of having the Flying Man, dad, what it means?"

Quite a stir got the people up to their toes, as rumors of the flying man coming to America's shores have reached the USA.

In a short period over the memo it's laughed like a duck in the papers. The good news established that Aaron's appearance wasn't matching with people's opinion in America.

Many days had passed; Aaron relocated to peripheral. Currently he's listened what Glen is clarifying:

"It shouldn't raise suspicion to others that you're able to fly, Uriel! As they could cunningly take advantage of your extraordinary gift: yet you've to beat World records in sport, specially running steeplechases, and competing in air acrobatics!"

Aaron's training was conducted under Brandton and coach supervision; have lasted longer than they anticipated.

But Aaron didn't struggle, for he's taken obstacles of any height. In Circus arena he flew in trapeze advantageously over the dome.

These complexities of rehearsal have taken place in desert, primarily at dawn.

Only for the fact, in the words that weren't practiced; Jimmy slips it of a tongue: "Aaron! Sorry, I meant Uriel! Don't move boundaries that physically possible only for the flying man! We can develop tricks and show to spectators that would-be rather magnificent! You've to perform warily, especially preparing for hurdles. For instance, you must count when jumping, with nor more than fifteen feet high. And if you perform air gymnasts, then use a safety net, or fall on trampoline!"

Coach and Brandton have trained him for steeplechases with the best runners at Gym.

Preparations have taken place in deserted area, away from those snooping eyes.

Often Aaron's shown unlimited ability, succeeding in great-arranged preparations.

Still was recalling when he ended up in Monastery, Buddhism habits have taught him survival techniques.

Despite tough measures, he never complained of be tired. Aaron's coaches are having forced him to simulate fatigue, and shortness of breath.

During intermissions, with awareness to maintain interest of the public, Aaron would perform as a proficient acrobat. Despite short-term training, Aaron couldn't instantly show his superiority in all its virtuosity that he possessed.

Most of the time Uriel was covered with sweat, and exhausted from the trainings.

While Circus management prepared and specially designed outfits for Aaron's routine, and for other performers since they've traveled outside America.

Glen meantime, was interested in horse's routine; but these tricks of somersault overhead by acrobats that be executed, haven't bemused him.

Days would fly one after another, so fast; Aaron naturally, was wondering about Chatelaine senior's displeasure toward him. Glen, his son, always restrained him.

Many times old Chatelaine interfered in Aaron's rehearsals, at the Circus arena: 'Uriel, you must put more energy! Do a quadruple somersault!'

Despite Glen was fed up with his dad's intrusions, but him being polite: "Don't worry, dad! The Flying man was trained well. And I didn't spend your money for nothing, dad, all will be paid off. Now I invested in a Baseball team! I've already launched an advertising campaign and funded that, on a high scale, it's unusual even for the USA!"

Media meanwhile, didn't know much about so-called Uriel, and have portrayed him in newspapers, magazines, even on the posters, or billboards: "A world of miracle be found: by a man from China's wild mysterious province!"

Early enough USA public reviewed traits, and knew Uriel better than their own Congressmen. The fans would rave to sneak all sorts of ways to see Aaron be known as Uriel.

Meanwhile, some of those invited players who were viewers knew would increase their bets... 'Uriel Invincible', with this title Aaron has advanced for interviews with the Media.

Becoming a worldwide in sport Aaron went straight, to have earned the title 'Uriel Invincible' with triumph, over his extraordinary performances in Circus.

Virtually every weekend, during the evening sessions at Circus arena by, which Aaron's performances made audience are calling him 'Great Uriel Invincible'; this has brought him even greater success in America.

From the time when Aaron arrived in America, and have got backing of touring over all major cities in the USA.

Sensation of the fact that laid in his brilliant routines was in the Circus tent or at showground; plus success has followed him across America and beyond.

Though management became exhausted from excuses of those spectators who couldn't imagine seen, when they come to the Show. It seems each of Aaron's performances under dome, considered to be unique.

Aaron's success sustained under guidance of his promoters, but was in the urgency to give his body a healthy weight, and attempted the best of his ability to conceal the secret of being 'The Flying man'.

Constantly set against all the less diverse betting, Aaron named Uriel played fair; though there was grumbling turn of deception towards him.

It looked the time come to make it all happen, yet Aaron's triumphs have continued.

Meantime, week later, upon arriving in USA from the tour, seen Brandton and Glen were having a chat in the office of Circus.

Resulted of the decision they've made on agenda; Glen held: 'It's time for possibility it's what I promised my old man. We need new tricks to broaden interest of the audience on his performances: Uriel has to suffer defeat!" Implied Glen.

Thus, ridiculous decision makes Jimmy shaking his neck: "If you insist? It's settled!"

The Circus Trust, to which Glen has amassed unprecedented in the history of its profit from performances by those entertainers, counting Uriel.

One of these evenings, after his usual routines, Aaron be seated in his dressing room, is wearing an outfit, in which he has performed every weekends at the Circus Arena.

More often then not Aaron was lost in his thoughts, and remembered the whole thing that he has undergone to get, where he is right now: "Ever since I've gained my freedom, and stay firmly on my feet. Still, I must learn who I'm? Me will connect with my friends in China, and never to be separated from them!"

For the time being, Aaron has already visited many cities in the USA. He's performed on tours in Central America, even appeared with his routines in South America.

For all this, thanks to Chatelaine and Circus Trust that have amassed unprecedented profits in the history of their Circus, and been Aaron's promoters.

Chatelaine senior, got involved twice as before with the Show; has watched Aaron closely; yet thought: "This man, Uriel, perhaps will talk soon of increasing his fees?"

Although this old man was mistaken, Aaron wasn't infected by greed. On the contrary he's spirit been free, aimed at great things; profit was far-off his mind.

After his performance at night sessions, in the Circus, Aaron was known as Uriel, would go relaxing in his hotel room.

For his next routine, it would move the Circus along with Aaron to new locations.

At some stage of the performances, and moving from one city to another, without Aaron's noticing the difference between the lodgings or apartments.

Among his triumphs of performances in the US Circus, Aaron has never forgotten his loyal friends in China.

Once he began earning big bucks in America, directly to the far corner of China have flowed parcels and cash for them, nearly every month.

Many nights Aaron wasn't asleep, thinking devotedly: "This time around, I didn't forget to buy a shawl and jewelries for Wu Lan? No clothes for Song Chuan, I'd rather send him a tube he'll learn to play music! As for Yuan Lu, elegant girl's dress! I wouldn't forget a gift for Wu Tang, I'll send him ornate pipe, filled with tobacco!"

Aaron called Uriel, regularly received letters from friends in China, and seen their mails have been filled with love and gratitude for him.

One of these days Aaron sits on sofa, and is reading one of their last letters: "Old Mr. Wu Tang has recovered. We all are waiting for your return, Xian Wei..." Suddenly Aaron stops reading. He raises his head; and quivers with it.

Spur-of-the-minute he's into thinking. He's look expressed being opposing, as if something held him back: "I'm not yet ready to drop all, and fly to the mountains of Himalayas, where 'orchid-epiphytic' flower is growing? For I need to help Circus employees and other folks?"

Neither fame, nor money change Aaron's character; on the contrary, it's opened up to fully and revealed decent side of his human warmth.

Chapter 24

MANY months have passed since Aaron arrived in America. But one night, during evening programs at Circus, he succeeded in the most difficult routine he has ever performed.

Minutes later, to Aaron wonder he has noticed a woman in a first row seat from the stage. She excitedly observed him; and has folded her arm on the balustrade, while she's been staring at him.

On a whim Aaron began thinking: "Her face seems is familiar to me? Yes, this woman looks like my mom? I remember Christi's cared for me as a child, when I was sick. Is she my sister? After all, Christi lives in London, and couldn't arrive in USA? Or she did?"

At some stage of his next performance at the arena, Aaron bowed to spectators repeatedly, turning from left to right, harmonized to the masses that have endlessly applauded him.

After his act was completed, he has nervously fled through the passageway.

As he's reached his dressing room, where began meditating amidst his thoughts: "Maybe I was mistaken? Is she really my sister, Christina?"

Shortly after, while Aaron gets undress behind screen-wall, still meditating, when the assistant knocks at his door; he's answered': "Come in!"

Prior to help him to strip from outfit into regular clothe; the assistant has brought a business card from someone, and handed it to Aaron.

On this business card be printed 'Miss Christina Dalton. Copywriter-Publisher, London.' The note attributed: a pen, aplomb, and big chunk of calligraphic across her stylish handwriting.

Involuntary vague of memories have flooded Aaron's mind, in which nostalgia of his childhood with flashes like film fetched his mind: "Christina Dalton? Yes, I'm not mistaken, she is my sister!"

He knew it promptly: 'Oh, my God! This is really Christi!'

Resulting Aaron has hurriedly dressed up in casual cloths; and left the hotel-room to catch her, before she leaves.

Meantime, Christina hasn't left pavilion, instead her been on open-air. On Aaron's approach a woman made vogue smile, it's received sound of her tongue-in-cheek: "We cannot talk here! Uriel, I'll wait for you near entrance, C.W. after you free from duties!"

Aaron didn't realize, when saw outside so many cars, which have fenced around the Circus tent. That crowd recognized so-called Uriel instantly; and all of them began applauding him.

Aaron's stopovers from surprise devotion, with a habit of bowing for those fans; besides he is thinking: "That's it! They know who I'm?"

Up-to-the-minute, she was waiting for him, but frowned once encountered a crowd with Aaron's fans encircled. From a shock or after, he is unable to think clear, listened what his admirers screamed.

On the spot, Christina began yelling: "Taxi! Stop here! Get in the cab, Uriel, quickly!"

Finally, Aaron sees her; then they both are stepped getting fast in the taxi. It's when they're seated in the cab that is out of nonstop buzzing with the stream of cars on main road; Christina turns to face Aaron, with a hardly visible smile; her tongue is in cheek: "Do you know who I'm Uriel? Or should I call by your real name, Aaron Milton Dalton?"

Aaron nods with his head: "Yes, it's me, Christi! I recall, when I was sick, you took care of me. If only I knew back then, sister, that we're to be separated?"

Christina slightly pulls forward, and bends in front of the cab driver, telling him: "Can you drive us to the hotel in Manhattan, please?"- As she turns back to face Aaron, and says heart-to-heart: "We've to talk about many things, Aaron?"

He nods his head in agreement; and plants a visible smile: "Yes, we sure do, sister!"

At this moment of time, as they've entered a fancy hotel-room that Christina occupied. It seems for them: like it's turned brother and sister back in time of their childhood, both have recalled how they parted twelve years ago...

Suddenly, Christina takes Aaron's hand, looks at him with tears in her eyes; it's special for them; and she kisses his forehead.

On this unique occasion Christina sees a chance; but began talking in a low voice: "Here, at last, I've found you, my little brother!"

Aaron in his turn isn't daring as to kiss Christina in the cheek. When they are seated down at the table, Aaron said: "Christi! I never forgot you, and have often seen you in my dreams,"- he takes a halt; and looks in her eyes. He then is telling more: "But how did you know it was me? Why haven't you written to me, or got in touch, before?"

Christina in her turn takes a deep breath, saying: "Aaron, I didn't write to you before, because I wanted to have more information, and to be sure it's you for real? For I was deceived many times! You my brother, I'm certain now! But if you've doubts, I'll show you portraits of our father and mother?"

Resulting she gets up of her sit, and walks toward the chest of draw, and take out a box; follows that she opens it up. In a flash she lifts a photograph from there, and is handed it to Aaron, in which he glimpsed a young woman with sad eyes. Beside her saw a smugly smiling burly man is wearing frock coat with sash of blue ribbon.

Aaron couldn't resist curiosity, and has asked: "Do you think I become like our father, who's wished me been the best?"

She shakes her head, and has alleged in a tone of reproach: 'No! It's bad if you think so. I hope you great in your own way, Aaron! Nonetheless, wrinkles, abdomen on photo of our dad...'

She became silent; a look up at Aaron haughtily, as if Christina has believed in what she's said: "Old age is no one's dignity. Our father was a decent man, Aaron!" She clams up.

Taken a deep breath; Christina moralistically declared: "Look, this is what I meant: our dad had a 'lively charm'. In his and mother's veins flowing blue blood, and they come from most honorable families in England!"

Just now Aaron's interrupted her; is looked amazed: 'Wow! What a sensation? So, in you and me is flowing noble blood? I seem to have done nothing of this sort to deserve it? Or can be reproached?'

Christina instead, said with sense of annoyances: "Aaron, not, really! Our dad was a respected citizen, a believer, and a wonderful host. And he had left you enormous fortune. Sadly for us, it had greatly made our guardians envious, as a result, they ruined you, that's exactly what detective Greenwood proved?"

By quirk of fate, Aaron slowly began to understand, what his sister was referring to.

She has inhaled gulps of air, and said: "I'm not surprised. But it did awfully upset me. What our papa, Sir Dalton, would say, if he knew that his son performs in a Circus?"

At this moment Aaron broke in, and deals with her: "Do you know, Christi, all the terrible things that happen to me? I was almost kidnapped, when guardians put me through hell. In the end, however, I don't see anything shameful in my line of work as a performer! It's an honest job, and I make a lot of money out of it!"

Christina stays quiet for a moment; it seems is unhappy: "Circus, of course, cannot be compared with the gangsters that can kill you without a reason?

'You must reflect on be the son of a Lord, from UK. All you need to know is our reputation highly respected over there. And you'll be well protected…"-

Not giving an opportunity for Aaron to object; Christina reveals more: "I know the secret of your success, it's the ability to fly, isn't it? You a human, not like birds or insects being flying? I saw you flew away from us, when we were in China. This violates all dignity of the human race? Aaron, but most importantly for us your habit of flying simply is threatening! I read it all in Chinese newspapers, where many passengers saw you in-midair, from the airplane?"

Aaron wants to protest; as directly he began touching upon issue of Wu Lan: "Christi, you can say anything you like, but Wu Lan thought I was a 'Demigod' in China!"

This time, she's interfered: "I know what you're going to say, but it's crucial for you to recognize, they've created and turned you into a flying monster? Yet, mistakes must be fixed, don't you agree with me, Aaron? Lucky for us, in England no-one knew about your past. I've made everyone to believe it you studied in University. Our friends rectified…" She stops talking; is taken a breath, and ongoing: "Please, Aaron, you must allow your condition be restored, for your sake and my! Rumors have it that surgery procedure can fix your health?"

Aaron intrudes, and said: "Did you know, Christi, I studied the ways as Buddha had, and he quoted 'Rumors are created by haters, spread by the fools, and accepted by idiots.'

Christina interrupts be upset: "Are you calling my friends idiots?"

He tries being silver-tongued: "Christi, don't take it the wrong way! What you're complaining me be the flying man?"

"Yes. As I was saying, you must become normal! Regrettably, this mad scientist has made you into flying man. What was his name?"

Aaron instantly badges in: "Dr. Spurt, called Hui Wei, by a Chinese name!"

Christina meantime, breathes in and out; then gestures her head: "Um, yes it's Dr. Spurt, so his Chinese name was Hui Wei? Unfortunately, he doesn't exist anymore, something awful has happened to him. I've read he wanted to create a flying division? Somewhat in experiments have gone wrong! Rumors have it that he jumped up to the ceiling, and smashed his skull. He was bleeding in the brain, but died, admired by many in his death, as the greatest scientist!"

Hearing of grave news, Aaron became solemn: "I don't think Dr. Spurt was mad. I truly believe contrary, your Mr. Fiend alongside Mr. Evildoer are mad people, and dangerous too! I want see them be rotted in jail!"

Christina intrudes directly: "Other doctors too can handle the risk. But if it goes public, hardly anyone will help you? And so, the only way for you out of restoring your health: it is surgery procedure! Vice-versa, you'll never resort to flying, even if 'your eyes drowning a child'!" She became silent; and is hardly relaxing.

Next she starts an argument: 'Now, listen to me, terminate your contract with Circus as soon as possible. Forsake a gypsy life that you exploited, and rather begin a new live with me in Britain, please?'

Aaron seems is speechless, and having a confused look: "I'm bound by Agreement with Circus. And, I cannot comprehend, Christi, why you against me being a Showman and athlete?"

Impulsively Christina cuts his words: "The family honor is more valuable than your career in Circus, brother! Prestige is highly regarded!"

Aaron immediately takes a lead: "I'll tell you another Buddha quotes - Let us Love not in the word, but in truth and actions."

Christina suddenly raises her hands, and makes a gesture, as if cuts the air to stop the argument. She then takes gulps of air: "I think we, in any cases, hereby will pay off any amounts for the penalty to the Circus. How this sounds, Aaron?"

Her words at last have struck a cord for Aaron; he became silent. For he's not yet aware of his sister's disposition, since their reunions was brief.

Aaron in his turn responded in a quiet voice: "Christi, I oppose to your idea. And I think we've to warn my boss Mr. Chatelaine, agree to a farewell, and discussing further all the details with him."

Christina, contrary has deprived of sympathy: "I disagree! No, Aaron, it will be a big mistake!"

It has sunk to Aaron suddenly; and he interrupted her. It seems him be dubious: "You know what I think, Christi, it could make others suspicious, where else the Flying man was involved in? You don't realize the consequences? My disappearance can set other people on a wrong path, and they'll go to search for me? I'm sure of it!"

She is disagreeable: "Do you know how many journalists are interested in your life-story, and dying to invent shameful fictions out of your past? If God forbid, they find out the truth about you, or us be noble? We'll be ruined! It's grown been scandalous situation, and we've to deal with it? I suggest, you and I must leave for London, immediately!" Christina stops talking for a moment; then is ongoing: 'I have already booked tickets for our flight. Aaron, go to your hotel-room and pack your things, then come back here!'

She's become quiet, in a flash; and looked in Aaron's eyes. By taken profound breathes; she has made a suggestion: "Be the Flying man working in Circus, you can inform their admin, before we leave with a simple call. The rest of your problems can settle Andrew, it's amazing what a bright personality like he's got?"

All of a sudden, Aaron felt as if now was trapped by his sister, and stared like being demoralized. He then began shaken his head, as if is opposing: "I can't, Christi! Today I've a free evening, but tomorrow it's scheduled for my performance, since the tickets were sold out earlier!" He discontinues; sees is taken a profound breath.

Christina is challenging, said with pride: "Maybe, all is needed to return those audiences money they paid for the tickets? And the situation would-be resolved! Then you can abandon your weird act! Dwell on it, you've provided the Circus executives by large amount of money long enough, with your performances."

The situation seems be unresolved; Aaron needed one thing to finish their hopeless conversation; thus he's talking on a whim: "I've responsibilities, and will come to see you, when I'm free! However, I'm not sure, when it will happen?"

Christina reminds him: "No later, than by tomorrow midday, Aaron!" She halts of talking, is putting an act; bows her head, and looked at her wristwatch. Next she lifts her chin up; and is revealed: "Tomorrow the airplane is leaving for London at 3 p.m. NY time zone. As you can see, we've little time left? Go, and pack up your clothes!"

Christina takes rest for a minute; is breathing in and out profoundly. This time around she declares:

"Now, I'll tell you briefly about a Circle of friends I'm acquainted with, who will be your links too, when we arrive in England!"

Chapter 25

AT the same day, on the verge of darkness, a remarkable warm night reached the Metropolis. There's come into view avenues then freeway follows in New York, where Manhattan and Broadway were filled with colorful streetlights.

Up-to-the-minute Aaron is in the direction of his flat from Christina's Park Avenue Hotel. On the way he has reflected what to make, of his sister's ultimatum?

Coming within reach of guesthouse ingress, where Aaron stayed in; he's still remained alfresco, for a minute or two, to distinguish the whole situation.

Walking to his room, at entrance near the kiosk, he's spotted a young woman, well-dressed, in a fur-coat. Her eyes seem be bloodshot, feasibly from excessive crying, although woman's expression read of thrill. Without shame, she's approached Aaron; in hoarseness voice, like she's at the brink of crying:

"Mr. Uriel! I was waiting for you, when Circus afternoon show ended. I've tried get in touch with you, but you left with a woman?" She stops talking, as if has felt that said too much. Yet, this woman is boundlessly talking: "How lucky that I've found your address in office of the Circus. I came here directly, and have decided to wait for you!"- Now she stops word short.

The woman halts her breath for a flash; this gave Aaron an opportunity to observe her. Despite wearing make up, she is appeared exhausted.

Suddenly, she began crying, then promptly resumes talking: "My God! You cannot imagine, sir, what I went through? Hour after hour have passed, but for me every minute counts..."

For a moment he became sympathetic to her distress: "Maybe you're distressed from staying outside my door? I don't get it?"

The woman shook her head. It's not unusual that visitors; fans or followers would approach Aaron, thus he's used to it, although this woman wasn't like all the others.

A minute ago, they've come within reach of his hotel-room. Aaron is seen rushing to open the door of his room, and invited her to enter inside.

Switching on the light, it appears she's wearing expensive mink-coat. Without taken off the coat, and a purse in her hand, the woman threw herself to the knees.

Aaron is apprehensive, and thinking: "Certainly, some deep personal grief has brought her here?"

He feels awkward; even so talk loudly: "Madam, what happen? How can I help you?"

This woman raises her head, still on the floor, and stated: "I'm a suffering mother!" She swiftly shushes. Except her next behavior has confused him, as she kept crying:

"Yes, you can help a poor mother, sir that is down on her knees, begging you!"

Aaron jumps in, and tries to lift her up from the floor: "Please, stand up, madam! For God's sake, sat down on the sofa! What is it?"

Although the woman doesn't move, and shakes her head: "I'd not get up, until you promise to help me, and put me out of my misery? I'm tormented." At this moment, she is crying aloud.

Aaron's speech slowed, as he is comforting her: "Of course, if I can. But you should know, madam, I'm in a hurry, and haven't got much time."

Abruptly she stops crying, lifts her head up, and looks in his eyes: "I will take very little time from you, though."

On a whim, he's raised the woman from the floor, and sits her in a chair. Spur-of-the-moment, she takes out a scented handkerchief with a lace trim, and attaches to her eyes, still is sobbing.

Next she began telling her life story: "Mister Uriel you a foreigner! Then, it doesn't occur to you how awful customs in New York is? No rich men can feel safe in here. Have you heard about the gangsters of New York?"

Aaron's felt alarmed, is blushing; then begun shaken his neck.

She goes on talking for a minute or two: 'No? Well, there were several major American groups of gangsters, and they're wealthy. These gangs have huge amount in Bank accounts; and without hesitation bribe the authorities, and patronize people.

'The worse thing is, Mafiosi group kidnapped thousands of children, in a broad daylight, on the streets, and demand ransoms from their parents!"

Now this woman became quiet; and has moaned: "I'm sorry, of throwing all horrors at you, and describe it in details…"

Now she is enhancing: "I didn't try frighten you, it's essential for you to grasp my hopeless situation!" She silenced; puts a handkerchief to her eyes, wipes clear tears; and extends of her taking:

"My name is Ellie Warren. My husband Mr. Warren is one of the richest persons in the US. But our greatest treasure is our daughter, Anne. She's only four years old. But she was kidnapped. Now she is facing a terrible death? Please, help me Mr. Uriel!" This woman began sobbing again.

Aaron on the spot is shocked after hearing of her tragedy. Even if he's nervous, but tried to lessen her grief: "Calm down, Mrs. Warren! And how I can help you? Here, have a drink of water!"

Taken some sips, her teeth are chattering on the rim of the glass. This woman gave a vogue smile, and is extending her story: "Thank you, sir. I'll explain everything. These mobsters have sent us several mails with a ransom of twenty million bucks. My husband would pay them off, but my brother has convinced him to wait.

'They will kill my Annie anyway, even if these gangs collect ransom!" Seen her shoulders are fidgeting.

Concisely she came to her senses; and tells more: "Matzo my brother, wants to buy time, and is hoping to find a way to save our child. But the Mafiosi's have bribed the police. Yet the Cops said that they're doing all they can!

'But they couldn't prevent attacks on the trail of bandits, who have kidnapped our daughter?" She halts of talking.

A woman then has sighed a profound breath. Turning her head back and forth, she spreads new evidence: "We, or rather Matzo, have turned to private detectives. Because my partner and I out of grief have completely lost our heads! He paid them big bucks, and we're able to find, where our daughter is? Though the police was pretending to be interested finding her anywhere, even in the Mountains area. I've received information that my poor girl was taken to Manhattan Downtown, on the six floors of the seventy-six stories skyscraper. Who would think of it? Now's the most important thing.'- She has delayed, while is watching him.

Unforeseen, she's exposed him: "Pardon me, rumors have it that you be able to fly? Is this true, Mr. Uriel?"

Aaron finds himself in hot water; is alarmed; but pretends to be cool: "I... is flying? No! What a weird idea? Why would you think that?"

A woman hit right on target, has succeeded in making him nervous. She's sensed, so opens her handbag, takes out a cigarette-case, and lights up a cigarette. She gestures to him thereafter: "You want to smoke?"

Aaron's tensely: "I don't smoke! I'm an athlete!"

She appears is making dim circles of smoke: "It touches on, and can resolve all, it strange, but incredible! You might think I'm in grief and lost my mind? But it wasn't my idea. Although one amid detectives came to a conclusion that you are able to fly, and it's be the secret of your success, mister Uriel! And don't deny it? You know something, sir, don't think people ignorant, they're highly observant and intelligent!"

Aaron has become more alarmed than ever; yet, doesn't know what to do.

Whilst this strange female, without noticing he's blushing, is put in picture: 'I'm a woman, but don't think me being stupid, quite the reverse. Mr. Fooled is a detective, and watched your performance in the Circus. And I've to say that he came to a conclusion: when took all boilerplate about the Flying Man, from China? After all, you're from China? Are you not, mister Uriel?'

Aaron feels as if is in jeopardy; subconsciously nods his neck up and down: "Yes."

A woman instantly prolongs: 'Besides Fooled said, the only person who can save your child is mister Uriel, but I doubt that he'll agree? And yet, I decided to come alone, and beg you for help!' Rapidly, she has made a movement again: falls on her knees in front of him.

Promptly Aaron held her back; then he's almost ordered her to: "Not again, please, madam, for God's sake sit! Let me see if I can help?"

He takes timeout to think in-depth: 'What if folks in the US have guessed that I'm the flying man? I don't wish to upset Christi, she is my sister, and the only close relative I have. But who want to be a loser, if gamblers are placing their bets on my failure it'll be resentment? Finding my secret, they could reveal the mystery of my blue-blooded origin, too?'

Reflecting on tough situation, he's said to this woman: "I need more time to think, I'll let you know!"

A few hours' pass since, Aaron rests in his hotel-room, is deep into thinking: "Soon my mysterious arrival will be revealed to the public?

'Evidence about me will be available? Most importantly a scandal happens? And gossips will affect Christina too, with her prejudices that Europeans are the best? What about Mrs. Warren, how I can fulfill her wish? A child is in danger, of course, she's counting on me, and of the Flying man, yet I can't bare to face the suffering mother?"

"Hardly anyone could notice me in the air, particular at night? I'll be flying at high altitudes. And in the end I'm leaving in the morning for England? But do I've time for another miracle?" Reflected Aaron on difficulties he's facing.

Later that day, at evening Aaron calls someone, it seems as if is adrift: "I'll be glad to help, madam! Sadly, at my disposal is very little time just two or three hours. And you should understand, I was urgently called to..."

She reacts rapidly; in a pleasing voice: "It wouldn't take more than two hours, Mr. Uriel! Our skyscraper located not far from here, next to where my poor child is suffering. The car is waiting for you downstairs. Say you agree? You wouldn't resist to mother's grief?"

Half-hour later the woman is met Aaron, in hotel lobby. As a respect, she firmly has shaken hands with him. Except her curiosity about his personal life has made Aaron feeling apprehensive.

Once they went through sliding doors; next stepped on the streets. Following one-another, they get in the car that waited for them, in front of the Hotel.

Outside developed picturesque night, where across New York are flashing lights lit full of multi-colors. There came into view many cars are speeding along highway, and pushing into traffic lane.

Passim appears Aaron is seated in the car. The girl's dad mister Warren seems is keen, but more like insane. Without getting of his sit, the man shook his hand; though his face flashed with angry smile, which gave Aaron chills.

Aaron finds in the car sat detective Fooled, his face tan; with slight scars caused by acne. There are Mr. Marcus, and Mr. Warren father of this kidnapped girl. He has a plainly facial features and close-cropped, grayish at the temple's hair. Now he gestured at Fooled and Marcus.

Fooled with a half-smile is revealed a secret to Aaron: "Please, Mr. Uriel, don't get-up! The luxury apartment we're going to is in skyscraper, this is the building that we've brought you on Mrs. Warren request."

Warren, says-so: "Thank you for responding to our grief, young man, now we've to talk!"

Aaron has found himself in a difficult situation; seem is hesitating, as if something held him back: "I... I cannot do it, I'm sorry! If this task is only to rescue a little girl?"

Fooled cut his words short: "Yes! You just have to act fast and decisive, the City plan and photograph of the building you'll get from me. Don't forget crossed marked, where the floor apartment's window located. Windows are always open in that design apartment.".- Fooled efficiently and clear has drawn plan of actions: "If today the child is not in our hands, it would become too late tomorrow? Come with us, mister Uriel, and I'll show you, where you can take off?"

Soon, come into sight the skyscraper where on flat rooftop, in a luxury penthouse someone's residence was located, with a desirable private garden overlooked.

Aaron on a critical moment was rushed; then stopover, and holds-on to a vertical pipe, while thought: "It was so long since I flew with pleasure? Its lightness in the air, as element feels spaciousness of freedom!" He's unexpectedly remembered: "What if I've refused to do it?"

Naturally he's felt peaceful, and thought of the past: "Oh, if only it was possible for me to carry Wu Lan in this free country, with beautiful flowers and trees? Why haven't I carried her into the Mountains to live? And there make love to her day after day? I'd have made nests on spreading trees. Or there we could live as a family: man and wife, together with Song Chuan and Yuan Lu?"

Hours have gone fast. Aaron hasn't got time to delay, seen in-midair. At some stage of the plan, he has flown across New York.

On this very moment there was no time for him to dream, it was time to react. Below, on the ground, Aaron seethed and rumbled a strange big city, and over his head, maybe polar Star has twinkled.

Bending head down he is looking from above, where the great Manhattan Island, with apiece a dark rectangle of blocks sees in Central Park.

Shortly he has approached Broadway that's route stretching across the Manhattan. Despite over the Hudson River occurs gloomy, it's reflecting lights within extents far, and are reaching many ships, coasters, the docks and marinas.

"Flying in then out of the window from over ninety floors skyscraper? This will be challenging, as a minimum, it's necessary to rescue a child, and snatch her from the hands of those gangsters?" Thought Aaron on his flight to aimed skyscraper.

Eventually he's passing Long Island where Statue of Liberty outstretched its hand. Distance from the horizon stretched the black surface of East coast on the Pacific, and moving stars amid steamship lights, within Eastern side...

A minute ago it's emerged close to late-night, Aaron flown across New York, with eyes closed, inhaling breeze of the wind, talking to himself:

"I sense a cold mouthful of clean air from the Pacific! It feels if pleasure fills inside, and I fly on altitude."

But he's unaware of numerous of people that noticing him airborne.

"It's not easy to find this place? Looking over skyscraper apartment's window, then to fly in?"

He's kept elevating. Surprisingly it has struck him: "Now I know where the apartment is? It's at Skyscraper the first window from the corner, on level 66?"

Flashing signals didn't disappoint: the window was open and lit into skyscraper apartment.

Aaron glances from above inside, and he is thinking: 'Let's have a first look over the window? I see a well-furnished room to be vacant. All is strange?'

On a whim he's felt safe, and has flown through the window, but tumbled on the floor. The doors have led to the right.

But Aaron turns left; saw the way leads to kids' bedroom, where the door remains vaguely open.

On the spot he began whispering: 'Is it a sign over there? I'll grab the girl; wrap her in a blanket, so she doesn't catch cold. And I'll move with her at the rear. What if anyone sees me? I wouldn't say a word, and will act fast by taking advantage of inevitable confusion.'

Across verge, Aaron next turns left; and quietly opened the door. After he turns left, there sees a child: in bed lays a little girl. Bending over it adoringly is a young woman; the little girl is not asleep.

Aaron has tossed and turned. Capriciously this child began crying, it is perceived voice: "Mama!"

A woman lifts the child from cradle, is held in her arms, and kissed it fondly. The child puts its head on mother's chest; seen girl's little hands hug around woman's neck.

Lovingly this woman touches this girl's hair: "Anna, don't cry, my baby, don't cry! Mama's here!"- She's engaged with the child; it seems is hesitant, and stood with her back towards Aaron.

Unforeseen: it's struck Aaron: "Now I've no doubt a young woman is the real mother of this child? Then, who was Mrs. Warren in my hotel-room? What she said about little Anna? Don't pull the child from the mother's arms?"

The woman scarcely rocked her daughter, warmly smiled; then turns see to Aaron. As she steps forward shaken hand with him, she is exclaimed honestly: "Doctor, you've come at last! We were waiting for you."

Aaron's found himself 'in hot water', and grasped it all. He stood with one foot on the threshold, does motionless, not known what to say, or to do.

To make a contact, this woman leads on talking: "Anna has cried in the morning. We thought she's with a headache or temperature?"

Impulsively the woman silenced; and has handed Aaron the child, she then said: "One misfortune comes, after another, doctor..."- Intuitively she's realized that mistaken him for a doctor; consequently felt been in a dodgy situation.

Aaron contrary is reacting uneasily: "Sorry, madam, I'm not the doctor here. Take your daughter back!"

The woman's turned pale, suddenly put her baby tightly to her chest, takes a few steps back with fear; she has asked: "Who are you? How did you get inhere?

'You not from those nasty gangs, who want to rob me of our treasure, my child, right?" She's carrying the child in her arms, whilst is attempting to turn on the alarm.

Aaron's felt been trapped, a jump in, and he gently grabs her hand, tries to prevent her from shouting: "No, please, madam, I'm begging you, don't call the Police!"

Aaron looked scared by extreme; so is thinking: "I'm unfit literally for such confrontations! And it'd have been best to turn myself in? No way! I would rather run into another room, and fly-away through balcony?"

Spur-of-the-moment, it gave the woman plenty to consider. Then she said: "All that's happened was a hallucination? Right?"

Aaron's grasped that was double-crossed, which involved wicked crimes by the Mafia; thus he wants finding out the truth.

Grasped that it's dodgy, he interrupts her, is schmoozing: "Please, don't be afraid, madam! Sorry, if I've scared you? But I can explain everything. Obviously, it's some sort of mistake!"

Impulsively she began screaming on top of her lungs; while saw her body is shaken: "Chase, come here, quickly!"- Her irritation transmits to this child, thus it's begun crying.

Unexpectedly, Aaron began hearing speedy footsteps, where a man in his 40s has walked into the room. Seen he's suddenly turned pale, whilst his wife stood between her daughter and Aaron, as if she is protecting her.

It's revealed the man was the real mister Warren, and this girl's father; when sternly and rudely, he said: "Who are you? What do you want from us?"

On the spot Aaron declares: "I'm Uriel from the Circus! And what's your name, sir?"

A man is holding the child, and hugged her. Next he peered into Aaron's eyes; be careful, at the same time genuinely amazed. He looked tense, has shaken his head; and begun talking: "I'm Chase Warren. Can I help you?"

Aaron is confused, but scared: "Sir, you said that you're Chase Warren?" He's realized the situation become extreme, and is getting out of control.

This couple finds what's happened on the spot was a shock; they're staring at each other, frantically for a jiffy.

At this moment of time, Aaron is finally convinced that he was deceived. In an extreme situation he is decided to open up, and tell the truth: "Are you for real mister Warren?"

This man has responded: "Yes, I'm really mister Warren! How can I help you?"

"Then, I've to talk to you, Mr. Warren!" Snaps Aaron, thus he is bewildered.

This time around, the man is confused, when looks at Aaron: "Okay. Let's go in my office for a talk, young man? Okay?"

Now all have become clear for Aaron, he reflected: "Oh, God! What have I done?"

Aaron nods; but sensed that found himself at stake, be tongue-tight; as he's thinking: "Oh, my God!"

Walking into his office Chase looks at him with interest: "Young man, you look familiar? Aren't you, Mr. Uriel, from Circus?"

Aaron bows his head; and without hesitation is reacting: "Yes, sir! And I'm the flying man!"

Warren's stretched a wide smile; is amazed: "It's awesome! Mr. Uriel, I've heard a lot of great things about you!"

He instinctively interrupts Chase: "Really? Thank you. But I've got involved in this affair, I'm sorry. Due to naivety those gangs wanted to exploit and use my ability to fly, for their own dirty dealings! I've entered here, from the neighboring apartment,"- Aaron stops talking; is taken profound breaths. He is ongoing: "I'm glad, I didn't become the instrument for these dodgy Outlaws in abduction!"

This time around, Chase shakes his head; and disrupts him: "I believe you, mister Uriel, I really do! You've probably been misled, and acted on a noble motive. In spite of be a talented acrobat, you look are innocent young man against those cunning and ruthless Mafia?"

Aaron intrudes, be like-minded: "Yes, you're right!"

Warren prolonged: "They've played on your virtue, to take part in crimes? I was told they hired an actress to adlib my wife. From what I can see you unaware of the US Law?"- Now he became silent.

Be taken a deep breath, Chase prolonged: "Mr. Uriel, if my wife was not near our child, a tragedy could be inevitable? Be in monsters hands, you've endangered my child's life; cause gangs without hesitation would enslave you too. And God forbid, you would-be jailed by-Law in US for kidnapping."

Aaron has felt ashamed; on the spot been worried: "Mr. and Mrs. Warren, please, forgive me! I didn't imagine the outcomes…"

Chase's intruded, and said: "You can't imagine the nightmare we've experienced, which my wife and I lived for months, be worried about our child safety?"

Chase's delayed; walks to his desk; takes out the envelope, and has shown Aaron anonymous letter, in which those gangs demanded money. He then has explained in details: "Gangs sent me threatening letters, but I've overpaid them a lot already. The more I give, the more cash they demand. Now they've threatened to abduct my child from the house. For our safety, I've moved upon height." This man has fallen silent. By taken a deep breath; he's ongoing: "There's another of their attempt have failed, from now on we've to watch the front door 24/7, with fear someone can jump over windows? What tomorrow will bring to us? I hired servants to monitor in and out coming folks. But who will guarantee us that no servants between accomplices' gang-kidnappers of the kids? For us, it seems is the only way to leave the USA!"

Aaron bends and looks at his wristwatch: a sudden hanged clock bang shows the time: it's on the brink of midnight. So, he gets up of his sit.

Chase lifts his right hand up, and points towards the door: 'The mobsters don't behave civilized. I must warn you, Mr. Uriel, since you've got involved with criminals your life is in a grave danger. Mr. Uriel, I advise the best thing for you, is to leave New York, even the USA!'

When next Aaron is on foot to the door, he turns to face him, and said: "Thank you, Mr. Warren, for the advice! I will do that! Everything you said, you were right, I should leave! Even acts of goodness can turn into an awful crime!"

At farewells, Warren shakes hands with a man that virtually has carried his daughter to abduction. He's forgiven Aaron all; rather looks at him with interest: "What will you do next, Mr. Uriel?"

Coming out of Warren's office, Aaron carefully is walking down a corridor; and is considering: "This terrible world leads the ability for me to fly. Lucky for me, I flew away from all horrors! Even far from Monastery, by, which I lived in fear to fall back in the hands of monsters? To hell Mr. Fooled, have could I be so blind, as the gangs tricked me? So far, many people took advantage of me: first Fiend and Evildoer in Monastery. Next that film director Shui Qing. Later was the priest Roberts. Followed by Glen and Brandton from USA Circus. Here I've got involve with gangs… To all of them I was only a passive instrument of their selfish purposes to get rich?"

It's awakened his honor, then he turns into maturing: "I'll never abide to greed! I've escaped before from cruelty! And I'll getaway from this incident too!"

Aaron is methodically thinking: "I'm still in danger? What if Mr. Warren or his wife had already called the police? Nigh in the building, projector of illumination only means that someone be on duty, lighting up for these mobsters?"

In a twinkle of an eye, Aaron decided to fly through one of the terraces, which was open, and opposite to the corridor, from Warren's penthouse.

Without losing time, Aaron flew across New York, where are seen dark obscured streets and traffic lanes. He's watched from above the entire green area of Central Park, where plants were neatly manicured.

Transiently Aaron landed in the midst of Central Park. He's postponed, made sure no one saw him. Next walking to the mall, there he is restored breathing.

On his escape some people, apparently have witnessed a drop of an object, or potentially a human?

Those men are discussing incident that, saw a person flying: "And we were not dreaming!"

When a third man joined them, is choking, he's asked to be seated nearby a chap: "You know what I think, this someone has fell down from a Skyscraper window."

Hearing the fourth guy replied: "Not someone, I think it was something?"- Then he turns to face Aaron; and resumes talking: "Young man, have you seen anything that occurred over there?"

Aaron pointed a hand up, is indicating aside: "Yes, I saw over there... I think, behind the bars, near Flower Shop, I saw something fall down!"

Before anyone recognized him, on a lucky occasion he walks off, with sigh of relief; is mobile, and thoughtful: "Thank God, that all has ended well!"

Chapter 26

MANY days have passed, from the time when Warren's affairs occurred. Aaron meantime, along with Christina, and Andrew, by now had landed in Britain.

A week later Aaron has received unexpected phone-call that have come from a prison. It's regarding specially the two prisoners: Ralph and Crofter that were put in one prison-cell for their crimes.

Aaron beside Greenwood arrived jointly at mid-morning in prison's Hospital, where those patients have got through earlier drama…

After inquiring with the admin, and searching for Bickering's whereabouts, they entered his ward. See are the prisoners looking desperate, but waiting for their turn of treatments.

Entering the hospital-ward, where Ralph laid in bed, Aaron seen him, but barely recognized the man he was. He lost weight, has appeared pale, like death being flying over him. Bickering's too spotting Aaron, and gave him a gesture to approach.

Aaron directly moves toward him, and stopover near his bed.

Ralph unpredictably, is low-voiced: "Aaron, my boy, thank you for coming! I'm glad to see you well, and grown up a fine man!"

Aaron contrary resolutely speaks his mind: "Mr. Bickering, I don't believe a word you say! Why I was called here? What do you want from me, now?"

Ralph shakes his neck; and began confessing in a low-slung breaking voice: "I realize how you feel. Before you decide, please, listen to what I'm going say?"

Aaron on the spot looks is apprehensive: "Okay, Bickering, talk to me!"

Ralph's ongoing: "Before you came to my ward, have you seen what department it was?"

Aaron began shaken his head; Andrew is repeated after him.

Ralph jumped in: "No? I'll tell you Oncology department!" He rests; is ongoing: "Aaron, I've lung cancer! Doctors gave me no more than three months to live,"- he's lacking to complete; it's appeared Ralph is gasping for oxygen. Ensuing he is pleading: "You probably wonder why I asked you to come see me? Well, before I leave this world, I want to confess, I'm a bloody sinner!" Now he began violently wheezing. After Ralph's subsided, he lifts his head, looks at Aaron, and said:

"I regret I've not got a son; but if I born one, I wish him to be like you, Aaron. And to my son I'd reveal, when I was young I've met a Jewish Scholar, who told in their religion were wise men. I come across one, who voiced Jewish quotes - If you already a sinner, then at least enjoy the sins." Look tears starts rolling down his cheeks, he said: "I beg for your forgiveness, Aaron!"

On a crucial point Aaron acts like is easygoing; seen his body bends over him: "Okay, Ralph, I forgive you! But, you hold on, maybe there's a chance?"

Ralph disrupts him; is ongoing: "I've undergone radiation-therapy! There's not a chance for me surviving. Cancer cells spread all over my body,"- he clams up; raises his head, and looks at Aaron. Then he's prolonging: "Goddamn it, you strike for me a chord of my exploit! There're characters of diverse ancestries, which tried to humiliate others less fortunate, like you were an innocent child. However, it makes us equal before death!" He halts talking.

Next is ongoing: "Aaron, I wouldn't go to make it! I've two things to say to you: one is an advice I know within my soul 'that nothing ventured is nothing gained, and that success and wealth never come easy or on a platter of gold', this is the only truth I've learned."- He rests; seems he's gasping for air. Then he is sustained:

"In China, I heard Buddha's aphorism - Be yourself. Because original worth more, than a copy!" He's suspended, seen struggles for air. After he resumes talking: "Now, son, grand a favor to a dying man: my appeal is just, as we speak, for Crofter. He was my life-partner! Promise me, not to charge him harshly?" Ralph's fall silent; looks with plead in his eyes. Next he moved his gaze to Andrew.

Aaron is concerned about him, and folds his hands on upper chest: "Ralph, I cannot promise. Just tell me, whose idea was it to get rid of me?"

Bickering is still gasping for air; then he's responded: "We were both guilty! We've maliciously misled others, due to greed! I'm glad that awful things didn't finish your life. You alive, and become the Flying Man! I knew your dad; he was a fine man, like you. If he were alive, he'd tell you idem: you're unique, because you can fly. Bravo, preserve this gift my boy, because God gave it to you!"

Couple days later, Aaron read in 'daily' that Bickering has died. It was evident, when he saw him last time in prison Hospital, it wouldn't be long until Ralph's departed.

Now its have passed over two weeks since those four: Aaron, Andrew and Christina arrived in London.

Meantime, Christina without delay organized a reception at Dalton's mansion that have attended the rich and famous, or 'cream of the crop'.

Later that night, after the party was over, she schmoozes with Aaron and Andrew in the living room, whereas they're watching television programs.

Suddenly Andrew is asking Aaron: "Do you like to have me as your brother in-Law?" He then turns and tackles her: "Do you agree, Christi?"

She's became heated: "You're not of a noble blood, forgive me for saying this,"- she stops talking; as has realized that said inadequate.

On a whim Aaron challenges her: "Christi, I thought about your demands…"

She disrupts him, and says in arrogant manners: "Tell me, have you decided going with alternative surgery in England? And recuperate to be a normal human?"

In his turn Aaron's head angled, he is reacting: 'In Tibet I learned to pretend and hide my true feelings. Fortunately, I flew away from all horrors and monsters, be drawn far from Monastery.

'Although I lived in fear to be back in the hands of those monsters, and was lucky be able to fly, for it's an amazing gift that any person can only dream of? Paralyzed by fear with some sort of curse, I didn't defend myself. Now above all, I can preserve my life, not the way as ordinary people do? For I'm the Flying Man or Sky Lord as the Chinese called me! And I'll remain by this name, whether you like it or not, as long as possible! Because I've the ability to fly!"

She on a whim seems isn't happy, where their argument lead to: 'I demand of you, Aaron, to abandon fabrication of being the flying man, with the Circus act, all together! And stop...'

Before she completed her ruling; he disrupted her, alone is having a word to say: "Christi, a Greek philosopher Plato said something related 'God gave us two wings: one wing is love, and the second, bright mind. So that finally, one day we can fly to Him'!" Proceeding, he provided a vogue smile; unfinished, is said: "You know, Buddha's quoted 'Before you try to change others, just remember how hard changing yourself!' I'll tell more, I can't recall who said wise thing, sounds like this 'Money doesn't make us better humans! But if we can find true love, we will be very lucky'! Christi, I've found true love with Wu Lan. And tomorrow I'm flying back to USA, not to New York, perhaps, to Mid-West where it's close to the Pacific Ports." Be offhanded, he subsequently become silent, for a moment.

Up-to-the-minute, she shakes her head, like is about to explode. Not given her a chance to talk, he's signified: "Christi, I'll remain the Flying Man, by this name I was well-known in China. I won't lose my ability to fly, due to your selfishness! For it's the greatest gift from God to me!" He halts of talking. Looks her in the eyes; and he is taken deep breath.

She in contrast, tries to argue. Though Aaron disrupts her, and alone is indicated: "As for the fortune that I own, a wise man said, and me know in my soul – nothing ventured is anything gained.

'That success and wealth never comes easy or on a golden plate! That is the truth of life I've learned for years. So, I bid goodbye to you, my sister! Maybe we'll meet again, when you will improve?"

Aaron went to his room unhappily, is leaving Christina in disbelief, and wondering.

The next day, once Aaron has left for the Airport; at dusk Christina came in Andrew's room, and knocked. When he opens the door, on threshold she asks him to come to the lounge, for a talk.

Christina sees is motionless, but disturbed; and forgotten about good manners. Capriciously, she began yelling: "I refuse to your proposal! For the reason that now Aaron is my priority!"

Although she struggles to be calm cool and collective: "I must give you credits, Andrew, for your effort helping to find my brother, in that horror Chinese mental Institution. Where from it were able to make a person in their way, utterly disperse."

It seems Andrew is apprehensive: "Christi, I'll forget, what you said about me, in an offensive arrogant way! Only if you promise me…"

On a whim, she interrupts him, but sounds twitchy: "And if you keep doing such dangerous job, you'll lose everything, even your life, Andrew!"

Now Andrew is having a word, but with sarcasm: "Obviously, your brother, Aaron doesn't think ill of me, Christi?" He halts of talking. Stretches a hand, and bends forward three fingers jointly of his hands, as if he is making a point: "One, out of curiosity, are they in your 'society', to which you be drawn all like Crofter and Bickering? Second, in whatever evil they've acted toward both of you're. Do you supporting it?"

Christina finds herself in 'hot water', seems be concerned of Andrew's blames, mostly of shameful behavior in front of guests, earlier.

To shock him, she pretends to be repented. Resulting, she's assumed in a false, but sweet voice, as if pushed her tactics: "Andrew, please, excuse my hot temper. Aaron and you, of course, were not to blame. To be more specific, you cannot jump in one leap from one case of murder to another, Andrew…"

Her sharp words are preventing him from speaking, Christina hushed him be silent; when she saw an opportunity, and is taking situation in her hand instantly. By taken a deep breath, she opens up:

"Partly it's my fault, because you and Aaron were not ready for the High society. Andrew, you need to realize, if we want to be together, you should quit such dangerous job, you're involved in!"

Andrew didn't listen to her, contrary, made a suggestion: "Christi, and three, you know something, I'm tossing between flight to New Jersey, and staying in Britain?

'Here I'll be tackling your insincere Aristocracies? Don't be selfish, my dear!"

She seems is ambiguous, when disrupts him: "Andrew, that's a bad joke, if you tried to be funny, then you've failed!"

Suddenly Greenwood's expression has changed to serious. As a result, he is easy-going: "Damn it! I've realized it! I need more time to get use to. And we've to dwell on it? But I do love you, Christi, with all my heart!"

Spur-of-the-moment, he walks up to her, bows, and began passionately kissing her. As Andrew is touching her lips with his, synchronously he said: "It's late-night. I'm tired, and want to sleep. Good night, Christi, let's talk tomorrow?"

THE END